J FIC Matas
Matas, Carol,
Cloning Miranda /

APR 22, 2002   5.99   **hq**
BRUCE COUNTY PUBLIC LIBRARY

Scholastic Canada Ltd.
175 Hillmount Road, Markham, Ontario, Canada L6C 1Z7

Scholastic Inc.
555 Broadway, New York NY 10012, USA

Scholastic Australia Pty Limited
PO Box 579, Gosford, NSW 2250, Australia

Scholastic New Zealand Ltd.
Private Bag 94407, Greenmount, Auckland, New Zealand

Scholastic Ltd.
Villiers House, Clarendon Avenue, Leamington Spa,
Warwickshire CV32 5PR, UK

Canadian Cataloguing in Publication Data

Matas, Carol, 1949 –
Cloning Miranda

ISBN 0-590-51458-X

I. Title.

PS8576.A7994C56 1999   jC813'.54   C98-932694-2
PZ7.M37Cl 1999

5 4 3 2 1   Printed in Canada   9/9 0 1 2/0

Acknowledgments

Heartfelt thanks go to: my agent, Ashley Grayson, who actually suggested I do a book on cloning; my friend Perry Nodelman who critiqued the book in his usual perceptive manner and who helped me brainstorm; Dr. Nathan Kobrinsky, who suggested Miranda's disease and talked me through the symptoms; Eric Mercer, Ph.D., who most generously took the time to advise me on the genetic information; my editor, Diane Kerner, who is always a delight to work with; my husband, Per Brask, who listened to the manuscript chapter by chapter by chapter and kept asking "what happens next?" so I'd have to hurry and write the next bit.

And, finally, to my beautiful new little cousin, Miranda Baran, who inspired my character's name and the references to *The Tempest*.

*To Nathan Kobrinsky —
the world is a better place
because he is here to help.*

Chapter 1

"Miranda, why do you always have to be so good? You drive me crazy!"

Emma's words echo in my mind as I sit in English class, going over our conversation from last night.

Emma stood, hands on hips, face flushed, black curly hair swinging as she shook her head.

"Don't get so mad!" I answered.

"I'm *not* mad."

"Yes, you are."

"I'm just . . . frustrated. You never do anything *fun*."

"Why is it fun to stay out after our curfew? Our parents will just worry."

"So?"

"So, don't you care?"

"No!"

"Not at all?"

"No! They're my *parents*. They're *supposed* to worry. That's their job. My job is to be a teenager. Stay out late. Have fun. Come on. Bob'll drive us out to the trail. Hiking at night. It'll be awesome."

"No," I said stubbornly. "My parents trust me. They'd be frantic." I got onto my bike. The two of us were standing just outside Sue's house. Sue's older brother Bob had suddenly got this idea for a hike. Sue begged him to take us along. He was just humouring us anyway. I could tell. He didn't want a bunch of kids with him and his friends.

"We're not wanted anyway," I said to Emma. "Bob's just teasing us. Now, are you coming or not?"

"No, you go ahead," Emma sulked.

"You want to ride home alone?"

"No."

"Then come on."

"You make me so mad!" Reluctantly she got onto her bike.

As we rode I tried to calm her down. "I have an important rehearsal tomorrow," I reminded her.

She sighed. "I know. But you'll be great at the recital."

"Great isn't good enough," I muttered. "I

have to be perfect. And that means practise, practise, practise."

It was dark so I couldn't see her rolling her eyes but I knew she was doing it. Still, I *did* feel I had to be perfect. Nothing less would do. It was expected. I had the lead for my dance recital. What if I tripped? What if I lost a count?

"Listen to yourself," Emma chided me. " 'I have to be home on time, I have to get A's in everything, I have to be perfect' . . . no one's *perfect!*"

She was right, of course. That's why I loved having her as my best friend. She was the only one around me who didn't *want* me to be perfect. For a split second I wondered if she was right and I was too much of a goody-goody. But I didn't like to dwell on that too much.

"It's no wonder my mom loves you so much," Emma complained. " 'Miranda's such a good influence on you' . . . "

"See how reasonable *my* parents are?" I grinned. "They like you because *I* do. And they've never said you're a *bad* influence on me even though you are."

"I *try* to be," Emma corrected me. "I never succeed."

* * *

So as I sit here, paying no attention to what's going on in class, I can't help but think about what she said. And I can't help but wonder about it. I mean, Emma's parents are pretty reasonable — but that doesn't matter to Emma. She does the opposite of what they want just to make them mad. And when she *really* believes they're wrong and she's right, she'll lie or cheat to get her way. So, I wonder — why is Emma the way she is, and why am I the way I am? I guess what I really wonder is, why am I so good? Is it bad to be good? Am I a real teenager or just some kind of fake? Maybe I should practise saying no to Mom and Dad just so I can be more normal. I have to admit I'm starting to see myself as a little weird.

"Miranda? Are you with us?"

I just about jump out of my skin. Mrs. Dromboski is talking to me.

"Yes. Yes."

"Could you share your thoughts?"

Tell everyone in class what was going through my mind? I don't think so.

"Your thoughts, Miranda. After all, we are discussing your namesake from *The Tempest*. What does Miranda mean when she says, 'How beauteous mankind is! O brave new world, / That has such people in't?"

"Well," I blurt out, "she thinks those guys are hot. And it's cool that there are so many of them."

The entire class breaks out laughing.

"Hot," Mrs. Dromboski repeats. She smiles. "You're right, Miranda, as usual. That's *exactly* what she means."

See what I'm saying? I can't even get into trouble in class.

School finally over, Emma and I hurry out the front door.

"That must be my mom." I grimace at Emma. I can barely see the car through the mob of boys surrounding her new Mercedes convertible.

They step aside as I walk up and I slip into the front seat. "Let's go, Mother," I say, under my breath.

She waves at the mob, rather like a queen waving to her subjects, then burns rubber as we leave the crush. I roll my eyes. "Honestly!"

"You can be a terrible stick-in-the-mud," she smiles, her long hair whipping in the wind. We're often mistaken for sisters — tall, slim and blonde with blue eyes. We even dress similarly: tailored jackets, cuffed, slim-cut pants, freshly ironed shirts and, of course, penny loafers. I don't see why she had to buy such a flashy car. But she says she likes it and that I shouldn't be so self-conscious.

We arrive at the dance studio and I hurry into the dressing room to put on my costume. Most of the girls are there already in various states of undress. I'm not best friends with any of them but they don't hate me either. Well, maybe Cally hates me. She's so awkward and big and lumpy. I suppose her parents forced her to take ballet in the hope that it would make her more graceful, slim her down. But it's been a disaster for her.

She tries to make up for her clumsiness with a sense of humour, though. She starts to tell a joke as soon as I walk in. She looks like she hasn't noticed me but as soon as I hear the beginning of the joke I know she has.

"What do you call it when a blonde dyes her hair brown?

"Artificial intelligence."

I laugh along with everyone else even though I know she meant it for me.

My costume is a long black skirt over a deep red leotard. I play the scheming queen in a piece our teacher, Ms Leanard, choreographed. She's very happy with my technique but not with my interpretation. She tells me over and over that I have to reach down inside myself and find the dark places. But I'd like to know what rulebook on life has decided that we all have dark places? Maybe we don't — well, I can't seem to find mine, anyway.

As we troop into the rehearsal room Ms Leanard greets us all in that way she has, like she sees you but she doesn't. She always seems to be two places at once and I have no idea where the second place is.

"Ahh, girls, wonderful, let me check your costumes. Angie, that's a bit loose on you. Marlene, that's perfect. Michael, you look just right. . . ." There are two boys in our class, and one of them, Peter, is very talented. He plays the king.

"Now, Miranda," she instructs me, "I want you to take a moment before we start. Think of the cruellest thing anyone has ever said to you."

I rack my brains but those stupid blonde jokes are pretty close to the worst. I shake my head.

"Miranda!" Ms Leanard says, exasperated. "Everyone has had cruel experiences in their lives. A schoolyard bully, a girlfriend who has hurt your feelings. Come now. You need this to get into your character. You're still far too nice."

I think back quickly. All my memories are good ones. If anything awful did happen to me, I can't remember. I shake my head. "Sorry, Ms Leanard. I had a pretty happy childhood, I guess."

She throws her arms in the air in a dramatic gesture. "Then you must use your *imagination*. Imagine what it would feel like to be so angry, to hate someone so much that you had to plot to hurt them. You must *feel* it."

"I'll try," I promise.

"Fine, let's begin." She glides over to the table and puts in the tape. "Places, please!" She claps her hands. We all take our places. She presses the play button and the music blares out. The princess, Rachel, and the prince, Michael, open the first scene. I wait on the side, poised, trying to make myself angry.

That blonde joke was nasty, I tell myself. And I feel a small jab of anger. On the other hand, I think, imagine the taunts poor Cally must go through every day. She wants to lash out but she's probably afraid to do it to someone who'll lash back. She knows I won't. So . . . And then I'm not mad anymore. I sigh. Mother calls me her little psychologist. Ever since I was small I was able to tell why people were doing what they were doing. When I was five my parents had a party and Uncle Rob got drunk, and I had to explain to my Dad that Uncle Rob felt bad when he came to our house because he wasn't rich and successful like his brother. I remember them looking at me all astonished and my mother saying, "Meet Ms Freud." I didn't understand her so I demanded that she tell me who Freud was — and of course, that's when they started saying how brilliant I was.

My entrance is about to come up and I'm no farther ahead with feeling mad. I start to count down to my first jeté, watching Rachel closely since I must jeté over to her, when suddenly she goes all blurry. I blink my eyes. It doesn't help. Everything is blurry.

"Miranda!" Ms Leanard stops the tape. "You missed your entrance."

"I know," I whisper, "but . . . but . . ."

"What is it?"

"I can't see properly."

And *now* I feel something real. Fear. No matter how much I blink or shake my head it won't go away — everything around me is fuzzy and blurred.

Ms Leanard takes me over to a chair and

sits me down. "I'll go find your mother," she says, obviously worried.

"Hurry," I urge her. "It's getting worse."

Chapter 2

Mother thinks there's something in my eyes, like an eyelash or a piece of grit. I sit patiently while she pulls my lower lids down but she can't see anything.

"I'd better take her to the doctor," she tells Ms Leanard, and she hustles me into the dressing room, helps me change and has me in the car in minutes. "You can't fool around with your eyes," she says. "If there's something in there it could scratch the cornea."

Meanwhile, I am trying not to panic. The thing is, I'm never sick. When I say never, I mean never. I'll get an occasional sniffle or a mild sore throat sometimes but it's not enough to slow me down. Once I had a stomach flu and it was horrible — but it was only once. Emma calls me Superwoman because no matter what is going around the school, I don't catch it, and she does.

"Mother," I say in a small voice, "what is it?"

The blurring won't go away. It's just like being in the steam room of our country club. Everything's misty.

"Did it happen all of a sudden?" she asks.

"Yes."

"I don't know, Mira," she says. She only calls me that at certain times, if she's worried or if we're having a special moment. Obviously, she's worried.

I still go to a pediatrician and we have to walk through a jumble of toys and screaming babies when we get to his waiting room. I'm rushed into his office almost immediately because Mom and Dad own this clinic. In fact, they own health clinics right across the country — the Coburn Conglomerate — named after my grandmother because it was her money Dad used to build up this empire of his.

Dr. Corne greets me gravely, as always. The other pediatricians in the practice are full of jokes and seem to have perpetual smiles on their faces, but not Dr. Corne. I don't think I've ever seen him smile. He's not mean or grumpy. He's just serious.

"Let's have a look at you, Miranda," he says. "Is there something in your eye?"

"I don't know," I reply. "I was waiting for my

cue at dance rehearsal and suddenly everything went blurry. It's still blurry."

He peers into both my eyes with his small light. Then he checks my chart. "You were last here just under a year ago and you were in perfect health."

"That's right," Mother nods.

He examines my eyes again.

"Miranda, I'm going to order some tests."

Then, just as suddenly as it happened, it goes away.

"My eyes are fine again, Dr. Corne!" I exclaim. "It's gone away."

"Wait here for a minute, Miranda," Dr. Corne says and he motions my mother to follow him out of the room. They shut the door but it doesn't catch and it slides open just a bit. I can hear snatches of their conversation. "Tests, something there . . . impossible, I'm afraid . . . can't be . . . wait, be patient . . ."

The door opens. Mother walks back in, the colour drained out of her face. "What is it?" I say, alarmed.

"We're not sure, Miranda," Dr. Corne says. "But I can see something in your eyes, something that shouldn't be there."

"What? It's gone now. I'm fine."

"The cloudy vision is gone for the moment,

but we still need to do some tests. All right? They won't hurt."

I guess I don't have any choice so I agree. Since it's my parents' clinic I don't have to wait — they do all the tests right away. First a nurse takes some blood, then she gives me a slew of tests: CAT, EEG, MRI — who knows what any of it is — why can't medical people speak English?

It gets very, very late and I start to get hungry and grumpy. My dad shows up about halfway through the whole thing and, of course, he has a new teddy bear in his hand he's managed to buy before getting here. Anytime I've been bothered about anything — like when Princess Diana died — a new teddy has appeared almost immediately. This is a big brown one with very cute eyes and a really soft cuddly body. He gives it to me as I come out of the MRI.

"Thanks, Daddy." I throw my arms around him and he squeezes me in a big hug.

"You all right, Mimi?" That's what *he* calls me when he's upset. They can pretend there's nothing wrong as much as they want but as long as they are calling me nicknames I know I'm in trouble.

"I feel fine. My eyes went all funny but

they're back to normal. I'm glad I've never minded being stuck in small spaces," I add, looking back at the MRI machine.

"Some people go crazy after a minute in one of them," Daddy grins, "but you aren't afraid of anything."

How can I admit to him how scared I got when my eyes went blurry like that? I smile.

"That's my girl," he says. "I'm sure it's nothing. They just have to take precautions."

It's after eight by the time all the tests are finished and we go home. Mother grills us some steaks and I make the salad. We sit down to dinner around nine, in the kitchen. By that time I'm almost faint from hunger. About halfway through the meal the doorbell rings. When Mother comes back from the door it's with Dr. Corne. He looks serious, but he always looks serious so I try not to get worried. He often comes to the house to discuss the clinic with my mom and dad, so it's not all that strange to see him here. Still, my mouth goes dry and although I was shoveling my food in a minute ago, now I can't even swallow. I grab for a glass of water.

"Miranda," Dr. Corne says, "please finish your dinner. Your parents and I must talk for a few minutes."

Mother grabs onto the back of a chair. Daddy drops his knife and it clatters to the floor. What is going on? Do I have some fatal disease?

"What is it?" I say, my voice coming out squeaky and high.

"I'll tell you, Miranda, I promise. Just let me speak to your parents first."

He follows them into Daddy's study, on the other side of the house. I sit and stare at my food. Finally, I can't stand it any longer. I pick up the phone by the kitchen table and dial Emma.

"Emma?"

"Hi. How was rehearsal?"

"Something really weird happened. My eyes went all funny and my mom rushed me to the clinic and they did all these tests and now Dr. Corne is over here talking to my parents."

"Wow. You're not sick are you? You *never* get sick."

"I feel fine."

"Good." She pauses. "So why's Dr. Corne over there?"

"That's what I'd like to know. He said he saw something in my eyes that shouldn't be there."

"What?"

"I don't *know!*"

"Okay, okay, let's not panic," Emma says. "It's probably some sort of stupid cyst or something. Amy Horowitz had one on her eye. They did this little operation and that was that."

"This is *in* my eye, not *on* it."

"Right. Well. Let's not panic."

Every time she says that I feel more panicky.

Mother's voice interrupting us startles me so much I almost drop the receiver. "Mira, could you come into the study please? We have to speak with you." She's white, almost green. Now I'm really nervous.

"Emma, gotta go."

"Call me back!" Emma shouts, as I start to hang up.

"I will."

I follow Mother to the study. She takes my hand. Hers is ice-cold and trembling. I sit down in one of the big overstuffed leather chairs. Dr. Corne is standing by the fireplace.

"Miranda, I'm afraid I have some bad news."

Daddy kneels down on one side of me, and takes my hand. Mother seems frozen, standing just inside the door as if she's afraid to come all the way into the room.

"Miranda," Dr. Corne continues, "the tests showed that you have a tumour growing behind your eyes."

"A tumour?" I repeat. "Like cancer?"

"No, actually it's not cancer. It's a rare and pervasive disorder. Something is wrong with your blood vessels. They aren't growing right. They are producing tumours — you also have them in your liver and we can see the beginnings of more in your kidneys and in your lungs."

I don't speak. I don't understand.

"We're going to do everything we can to make you better," Dr. Corne assures me.

"But," I object, "I'm fine. I feel fine."

I look at Daddy. Maybe he can make Dr. Corne take his words back. "It's all right, Mimi. We can help you. We know we can." He pauses. "Mother and I . . . well, we can't believe it. You've always been so healthy we never thought we'd have to help you but we're ready. We've always been ready."

"Allan!" My mother's voice is sharp with reproof.

"I didn't say anything," he defends himself. "I just mean, you don't have to worry . . ."

I gaze at Dr. Corne. "Will you have to operate?"

"That will only buy us a little time. The tumours will still return."

"I don't understand," I cry. "Daddy says I'll be fine. But you're saying . . ."

"I'm just saying that operating on these tumours isn't a cure. But your parents have connections to the top researchers, the best specialists — in fact they tell me they know someone that can help. Let's see what he says before we jump to any conclusions."

"You see?" Daddy encourages me. "You'll be fine. I promise."

Mother walks over to me then and takes my hand. "Nothing is going to happen to you, Mira. *Nothing*." Her gaze is so fierce she almost scares me.

I am trying to take this all in. What they seem to be saying is that I have some horrible, fatal disease, and somehow they're going to save me. But you can't save someone from a fatal disease. So they must just be trying to make me feel better. My eyes fill with tears.

"I'm going to die, aren't I?"

"No!" Mom and Dad exclaim at the same time.

Dr. Corne pats my shoulder. "I know this is a terrible shock, Miranda. But the Coburn Clinics are the best in the state. They'll try everything." He pats my shoulder again and then he leaves. Mother sees him out. When she returns she and Daddy sit on either side of me.

"Dr. Corne doesn't know the man we've been working with," Daddy says. "You mustn't worry. Your mother and I were just shocked at first. But you'll be fine. I promise."

Daddy has never made a promise he can't keep. But how is he going to cure me of an incurable disease?

Chapter 3

Out of habit, I get up and go to school, although I hardly slept a wink all night. I lay in bed and stared into the dark. It's hard to imagine *not* being. At one point I felt a terror so deep, so overwhelming, that I snuck outside and sat under the lemon trees in the dark. I breathed in their sweet fragrance and gazed at the stars and tried not to think at all.

In the car, as Mother drives, I keep getting this image of tumours growing all over my body, taking it over. Mother, oddly enough, is in good spirits.

"I just spoke to the specialist," she chatters on. "Everything is going to be fine. When you get home from school your father and I will tell you all the details. I'm sorry we behaved so badly yesterday — it was a shock. We thought . . ."

"You thought what?" I ask. I have the distinct feeling she isn't telling me everything.

"Nothing."

"What causes this disease anyway? Why have I got it?"

She practically squirms then. "We'll tell you everything after school, Miranda," she assures me.

"Is there a name for it?"

"Von Hippel–Lindau," Mother answers.

"That's my disease? It sounds like some bad dubbed movie. Everyone will laugh at me!"

We arrive at school. Mother puts her hand on mine. "You mustn't worry. It'll be okay."

I shake my head and get out of the car. I think Mom and Dad are kidding themselves. They can't face the truth. Last night when I couldn't sleep, I wished I could have had all those colds and flus I never got. Maybe this is my payment for never being sick. Getting really sick all at once. I wondered if I should pray except we've never discussed God or praying or anything in our house — if there is a God wouldn't he/she get mad at me for just starting to pay attention now? Yesterday, I was worried about being too good. I'd happily go back to that worry now. I just don't want to be dead.

During lunch Emma and I go to the library. We drag Susan along because she's the biggest computer geek in class, and a good friend. Now that I know the name of the disease I don't want to wait until I get home to look it up on my computer. Susan has it tracked down in minutes. What I read makes me feel even more upset, although I didn't think that was possible. Blindness. That's what the eye tumours lead to. And a cure? None unless all the organs can be transplanted. The one good thing is it's not catching. That's a relief. Emma was definitely starting to worry about being close to me. Turns out it's genetic.

"Genetic," Susan muses. "That means you've had it since you were born."

"What do you mean?" I ask.

"It's in your DNA. It's part of you."

"Then why didn't I get sick right away?"

"It says here that it usually doesn't present until puberty. Sort of like a time bomb, ticking away."

"But I'm almost fourteen," I object. "I should have gotten sick two years ago."

"Maybe it started then," Susan says. "Or maybe the timer didn't work right away. What I can't figure out is why your parents are so surprised — one of them must have it too, right? Isn't that what genetic means? Inherited?"

"But they're both *totally* healthy," I say, puzzled.

Sue keeps reading. "This might explain it," she says after a moment. " 'Five percent are spontaneous mutations,' " she quotes.

"Which means, I suppose," I muse, "that my genes just went wonky completely on their own — and mutated into this weird thing. But *why*?"

"Who knows," Sue sighed. "Your mom could have been exposed to something when she was carrying you — or maybe it's just a fluke." She looks up from the computer. "Sorry, Miranda. It sounds bad, really bad."

"Susan, you have to swear not to tell anyone," I say. "I don't want everyone at school feeling sorry for me."

"Or afraid they'll catch it," Emma grimaces. "People can react that way, even though it's stupid."

Then she pauses, at a loss for words. I can see she has tears in her eyes but she doesn't want to let me see how upset she is. I *am* her best friend, after all.

"You guys go to lunch," I say. "I'm going to read this over again."

Reluctantly they both leave, Susan giving me a pitying look on her way out the door.

No known cure. No known cure. I keep reading it over and over. Mom and Dad must be grasping at straws. There's nothing anyone can do. But why did my genes have to go out of control like that? Why? It makes me feel so helpless. I've always been able to control everything, with hard work, practice, focus; I've always kept my life in order. Now it's spinning, spinning. . . .

I push up from the desk and go to my locker. I get my knapsack and head out of the school. I can't be here anymore. I need some fresh air.

It's a beautiful day; spring is just around the corner, so it's becoming hot. I look up at the palm trees as I stand on the corner and realize I don't know how to take the bus home. I've never done it. And I can't walk. It's miles to our house, which is on twenty acres of land just outside of town. Even when I'm bad, trying to skip school, I can't do it right. I reach into my knapsack and call Mother on my cell.

"Can you come and get me? I'm on the corner of Palm Drive, right near the school."

She doesn't ask why. "I'll be right there."

The sun beats down on my face. For a minute I worry that I forgot to put on my moisturiser with sunscreen this morning. Then I laugh out loud. What does it matter? I'll be dead long before I have to worry about skin cancer.

When Mother picks me up she seems almost cheerful. "I told you not to worry," she scolds me, "and I meant it."

I don't answer her. She's obviously lost her mind, from the stress and everything. I'm dying and she can't accept it. I put on the radio, loud, so she won't talk to me. When we get home Daddy is there, on the phone. When he sees me he hangs up and comes over to me.

"Listen, Mimi," he says, "you mustn't be so upset. We have everything under control."

None of us is in control anymore. They've *both* lost their minds.

"Come out by the pool," he says. "Lorna's made us some lunch." We go outside and sit down at a table with a large yellow umbrella over it. Lorna has fixed my favourite, spinach salad with grilled chicken, and she's made fresh corn bread. I can't eat. I feel sick inside.

"We've spoken to Dr. Mullen," Daddy says. "He works at a special clinic we own here in town."

"What special clinic?" I ask.

"It's not far from here," he says. "Actually it's only a few miles away. It's called the G.R.F. clinic."

"I didn't know you had another clinic here in town," I say, puzzled.

"Well, it's not open to the public. It's really a research facility," Daddy explains. "They've been doing a lot of work on transplants. And other things."

"You're going to give me transplants?" I ask. "But my liver? My *lungs*? You can't do that, can you?"

"You'd need a perfect match," Daddy admits. "But the doctor is sure he can find one."

I shake my head. I can't believe any of this. No one can have their lungs taken out and live normally. And Dr. Corne said the tumours would grow back, anyway. Something is wrong with my blood or my blood vessels. . . .

"We'll take you over there soon for some tests. Now finish your lunch."

We sit in silence for a few minutes. Then I say. "I looked the disease up on the computer. I know it's genetic. But neither of you has ever had it, have you?"

Mom and Dad stare at me. "Genetic?" Dad repeats. "But that would mean we — or one of us — passed it down to you. And I know we haven't. After all, one of us would be sick by now, right?"

Why is he asking *me*? He's the one who's

head of one of the biggest health groups in the country! I seem to know more about this disease than he does. Then I realize that he's probably been so busy trying to organize my treatment with this special doctor that he hasn't had time to really think it through.

"There's a small percentage of kids who develop it spontaneously," I say. "Maybe I'm just lucky."

Suddenly Mother gets up from the table. "Genetic," she mutters. She turns to go back into the house but her gait is so unsteady she almost stumbles as she walks. Dad shrugs at me and pats my hand. "Let me go talk to her," he says.

I sit by myself for a moment but then can't stand being left here alone, worrying. I get up and follow them into the house, through the double doors that lead straight from the deck into the foyer.

Beyond that is the living room. Mom and Dad are standing there arguing! I've never heard them argue before. And then I'm struck by how odd that is. Don't all families argue? Emma's certainly does and so does Susan's. I've heard them myself. I've been told about it. And yet this is the first time I've ever heard my own parents fight.

"There must have been a way he could have prevented this!" Mother is furious.

"I'll fire him," Daddy fumes.

"You can't fire him now, we need him!"

"She must have had it from birth," Mother says. "And he *missed* it. And he's checked her since. Why didn't he catch it earlier?"

Who is she talking about? Not Dr. Corne — I don't think. And how could he have caught it earlier? I'm not following this at all. Then Mother explodes. "I can't do this again. I can't! This wasn't supposed to happen!"

"Supposed to happen?" Dad challenges her. "We're way beyond that now, aren't we?"

"Are you blaming me?"

"Did I say that?"

"It sounds like you are," Mother hisses at him. "You blame me, don't you?"

"How could I?" Daddy explodes. "When we have Miranda — " and then he sees me. "Oh, oh, oh, Miranda, have you been listening to us?"

I nod.

They both rush over to me. Mother glares at Daddy. "You shouldn't have listened to us, Miranda. We're upset, naturally."

"What were you talking about?" I ask. "*Who* checked me?"

"Nothing," Daddy says, "nothing. Don't you have dance rehearsal soon?"

"Yes. Can I go?"

"Of course you can. Dr. Corne says there's no reason you shouldn't perform tomorrow. I keep telling you, you're going to be fine."

As Daddy drives me over to my rehearsal I ask him again what they were talking about. They've always been so honest and open with me but now when it really matters they seem to have stopped really talking to me. I say that to Daddy.

"You're right, Miranda, of course you are. Honesty has always been our policy." He pauses and looks like he's searching for what to say.

"We had you checked out very thoroughly by a specialist at the G.R.F. clinic when you were a baby. They screened you for every possible disease and well, they do genetic research, too, so they checked out your genetic health. And they didn't find this. So either they missed it or you're right and it developed later. Mother thinks they somehow should have found it."

"It all sounds pretty sci-fi," I say.

He smiles. "Not at all. It's common to screen for genetic disease these days. Our tests are just a little more sophisticated."

"Not quite sophisticated enough, though," I say, thinking out loud. Dad's face falls. He looks crushed.

"You're right," he agrees.

We are nearing the dance studio. "What should I tell Ms Leanard when she asks how I am?"

"Tell her that it's complicated, but you'll be fine. She doesn't need all the details."

Ms Leanard doesn't want to hear the details. She's delighted I'm back and the show can go on. She tells me to stop immediately if my blurry vision returns. The girls all ask me if I'm all right. I say I am. I really don't want anyone to know.

I change into my costume silently, unable to make small talk — I barely even register the other girls. Yesterday I was in perfect health, going for a perfect performance. Or so I thought. Today I feel dirty and ruined.

Ms Leanard starts the music. I make my entrance. And I find I'm angry. I'm jealous of Rachel and the fact that she'll live and I'll die. I'm jealous of all of them. I *hate* all of them!

When we finish Ms Leanard claps her hands in glee. "You've found it, Miranda. That dark place inside you. You've reached it. Good for you."

Good for me, I feel like saying. I have a fatal disease but I guess it's worth it if it makes my performance more believable. Instead, like the good girl I am, I smile and say, "Thank you, Ms Leanard."

It's not fair. It's just not fair. What did I ever do to deserve this?

Chapter 4

I lie in bed and stare at the ceiling. The conversation I overheard today keeps going through my mind. Dad explained everything, but not *quite* everything. What could Mother have meant when she said, "I can't do this again!" I asked her about it when I got home but she said that I must have misheard. I'm sure I heard it correctly — and why won't she explain it to me? So I asked Dad again. He said he didn't remember her saying that and even if she did she was so upset she wasn't making sense. It's their answers now that aren't making sense.

I can't sleep. I get up and creep down the hall so my parents won't hear me. Our house is ranch-style, the bedrooms and Dad's study in one wing, then the kitchen in the centre, after that the dining room, then a living room/family room with the pool and tennis court off that, and finally a more formal living room. Everything is done in wood, pale colours, southwestern style. It's a beautiful house.

I wander into the family room and go for the picture albums. I love to sit at night and look through our pictures, at all our vacations, and think about the fun we've had. We went to London last year and saw *Twelfth Night* and *The Tempest* done by the Royal Shakespeare Company. I laughed so hard in *Twelfth Night* I almost fell out of my seat. Maybe I'll be an actress, I think. And then I can hardly breathe, because suddenly I remember that I can't make plans. I don't have a future. It doesn't matter what my mom and dad say. The article said that there was no cure.

I flip through the pictures: me in front of the tower of London, me in front of the British Museum. A loose photo drops out. I pick it up. Me in front of . . . that's odd. I look closer at the picture. How did that get in here? It's me all right, in front of some big castle, but it couldn't be from the London trip. I look about ten years old. And where was it taken? Funny. I can't remember being there at all. And those clothes. Ugh. Did I really like to dress like that? Overalls? I don't remember ever owning a pair of overalls, even at that age.

I take the picture out and put it in my dressing-gown pocket so I can ask Mother about it in the morning. I look at my watch. It's 1 A.M. I turn the TV on quietly so no one will hear it — not that they would, if they stay in their rooms. I flip around until I find an old John Travolta movie.

* * *

My body is inside out, blood vessels, muscles, red and white, and everywhere are large black growths, they multiply, they expand, they are covering everything. I start to scream but where is my voice coming from? Where am I? Where am I?

* * *

I wake up gasping. I get up and stagger back to my room. I'm pouring sweat but I'm cold too. I head for my bathroom, and stand under the hot water, letting it wash over me, my mind, finally, a blank. Warmed through, I towel off and crawl under the sheets. I'm afraid to dream again and I can't fall asleep for ages.

"Miranda. Miranda." I open my eyes. It's Lorna.

"Up you get. Your mother told me to make sure you're ready. You have to go to the doctor's this morning. You'll just miss first period. What do you want to wear? The blue pants and blue jacket? It's a little cooler out today. Or what about your new brown top?"

"You choose," I mutter. Lorna has been dressing me since I was little.

She bustles around the room. "Tonight's the big night. Are you nervous?"

"Funny how when you know you're about to die, a stupid dance recital doesn't mean all that much."

Lorna drops the clothes she had in her hand on the floor. "What?"

"They didn't tell you?"

"They told me you were sick. But that you'd get better. *For sure*, you'd get better."

"They're lying."

I can't believe these words are coming out of my mouth. Neither can Lorna.

"Miranda, what's gotten into you? I've never heard you speak disrespectfully of your parents. And let me tell you, they don't deserve it." She is picking up the clothes as she talks. "If they say you'll get better, you will. Not once have they — " and then she stops, frozen.

"Where'd you get this picture?" She is holding up the picture that I found last night. It must have dropped onto the floor when I threw my dressing gown off last night.

"It was in the album from our London trip. It's a mistake, obviously, it's from years earlier. I was going to ask Mom or Dad."

"No, no," she says, "I'll put it back where it belongs. You just get dressed now."

And she's gone. Why is everyone around here acting so strangely? I didn't even get a chance to ask her which trip that was from. I get out of bed, go into my bathroom, wash my face and brush my teeth, then put on the pants, brown top and loafers Lorna left out.

When I get to the kitchen she has yoghurt and fruit waiting for me. I eat it standing. Mother hurries in. "Let's go, darling."

"Where are we going?"

"To the G.R.F. clinic we told you about. Dr. Mullen is expecting us."

"More tests?" I ask.

"Just a couple. He can use the results of the other tests. He needs a little more blood, and he wants to check you over himself. He's scheduling the operation for next week."

"What? What operation? It's *incurable*. I'm not going through some big horrible operation just so I can die later."

"Mira," Mother says, "don't be silly. We wouldn't let you do that. Come on. He'll explain everything. You're going to be cured, I've told you."

I shake my head, grab my knapsack and follow Mother out. I've gotten horribly behind in English over the last two days. I'm supposed to be writing an essay comparing Ariel and Caliban. I pull out my Shakespeare and read as we drive. Why I'm bothering I don't know. If I'm going to die I guess I don't have to worry about English assignments. On the other hand, if Mother is right and I'm not going to die, I'd better get cracking on it.

I laugh out loud.

Mother looks at me.

"Nothing," I say. "Everything just seems a little funny to me. Not really 'ha ha' funny, but 'so weird you have to laugh' funny. Never mind."

"Mira," Mother says, "this has been an awful shock for all of us — most of all for you, of course. I think you're handling it remarkably well. No tears, no hysterics. Sensible, like always. But Daddy and I would have expected no less."

If only I knew how to go hysterical, I think, it would probably be a relief. But this is the only way I seem to be able to react. So I return to my book and read until Mother pulls the car up in front of the clinic.

The clinic turns out to be a large three-story house on Canyon Road, set well back from the street, date palms lining the driveway. Red bougainvillea surrounds the front and a lemon tree just beginning to blossom stands in the small grassy area to the left. Mother leaves the car in the drive and we don't even have to knock — a nurse opens the door as we reach it. She is tall and very thin, with brown hair tied in a bun on top of her head. She smiles and I can tell she smokes. Her teeth are all yellow.

"Follow me, please," she says.

A middle-aged man in a white coat bustles down the hallway toward us.

"Ahh, look at you. This *must* be Miranda. Come in. Come in."

He has one of those posh British accents, which makes him sound very smart. His eyes are a watery blue and his hair is a thick wheat colour. He seems delighted to see me. Somehow I can't feel the same way. After all, I wouldn't be here if I weren't sick. Really sick.

"How's your vision?" he asks.

"All right."

"No more blurring?"

"No."

"Good. Good. Now sit down, Miranda. Jean here will take your blood while we talk." He ushers me into an examining room, sits me on the table. Jean rolls up my sleeve while he chatters on.

"You mustn't worry, Miranda. It's serious, but we can cure you. *Cure* you."

"But at school . . . the computer said — "

"Oh!" He laughs. "That's old material. We're going to get rid of all this with a brand new gene therapy we've developed. You may need a new liver. That's where the tumours are worst, which is a little unusual — normally they appear other places first. But you aren't yellow so your liver function is still good, considering. . . . At any rate, not to worry! We have a liver for you! And the rest we can shrink away to nothing."

"But . . . "

"No buts. If we need to replace your lungs and kidneys we can do that too. You've probably seen lots of doctor shows on TV — and you're going to ask me how I've found a perfect match. Well, that's my little secret. But by the end of the year you won't even know you've had this disease."

The nurse has taken my blood while he's been talking. He peers into my eyes with his light. "No, not to worry. It's unexpected, this, but we're prepared. Now off you go to school. Can't afford to get behind."

Before I know it Mother and I are back in the car heading for school.

"Wow!" I say. "Isn't he a little too much like a mad scientist? Someone should give him some calm-down pills."

Mother laughs, the first time she's done that since we heard the news. "You heard him," she says. "You're going to be fine!"

"But when did he find a perfect match for me? And don't you have to take drugs forever? On *Chicago Hope* . . . "

"No, he means a *perfect* match," Mother says. "So your body won't reject it. No drugs. You'll be as good as new."

"But *how* could he find such a perfect match?" I wonder.

"He just *has*," Mother says, her voice sounding a little irritated. "Don't keep asking, Miranda. Just be thankful."

"Is it because of Daddy? Did he find it in one of his hospitals? Someone who died? But don't they have to use the organ right away? Like right after the person dies?"

"Your father *did* help," she says quickly. "You know, with all his clinics and connections. And — I guess they figured out a way to preserve those organs for you . . . I didn't ask. But Dr. Mullen is the expert."

"I didn't know you *could* get such a perfect match," I persist. "Unless you have a twin or something."

"Drop it!" Mother explodes suddenly. "There is no need for these questions!"

I am so startled by her reaction I literally flinch. She's always explained things to me, we've always talked everything out. She's *never* snapped at me like that, she's always *encouraged* me to ask questions.

I stare at her. What is going on?

Chapter 5

I arrive at school in the middle of first-period English. Mrs. Dromboski is talking about Caliban.

"Shakespeare describes him as a 'savage and deformed slave,' " she says, as I take my seat. "Shakespeare is obviously not afraid of creating a loutish, ugly monster. Is there anything about Caliban to like?"

"I feel sorry for him," Emma says.

"He tried to attack Miranda," Susan scolds, her voice severe. "There's nothing to feel sorry for."

"He says he'll be wise," Emma counters. "He's growing. He's changing."

"A monster's a monster," Susan states flatly.

"Emma?" Mrs. Dromboski asks. "What do you think?"

If it weren't for the three of us Mrs. Dromboski wouldn't have a class, I think suddenly. No one else talks. I glance around the room. Everyone is in their own world — Selena is engrossed in one of her murder mysteries, hidden behind her Shakespeare, Tod is sleeping, Juan is doing Math homework, Michelle and Lara are sending notes back and forth to each other, Jason is staring off into space. . . . If it weren't for the three of us, the rest of the kids might actually have to pay attention. No wonder they're always complimenting us after class. It's not that they respect us, or even like us necessarily, we're *useful* to them. Why is it I'd never realized this before?

"Miranda? Are you with us?"

"The world needs monsters," I respond, "so we can hurt and despise them." Like me, I think to myself. That's what I am now. If people could see inside my body, all filled with tumours, totally disgusting, everyone would hate me, too.

Mrs. Dromboski raises an eyebrow and says, "Perhaps, Miranda, but that's a bit harsh, don't you think?"

I shrug.

After class Susan and Emma join me in the hallway on the way to Math.

"I just realized something," I say.

"What?" Emma asks.

"The rest of the kids in class — "

"Good work in there," Michelle calls out as she rushes to her locker.

"Yeah, great," Tod agrees as he catches up with us.

"What?" Emma asks me, as I haven't finished my sentence.

I glance at Tod and decide not to tell Emma and Susan my theory until we are alone.

"Nothing, never mind," I say.

"Where were you?" Tod asks. "You're never late."

I can't think of a good reason — I can't tell him the truth but I can't lie either.

"Her mom's car broke down," Emma volunteers.

"Jeez. Really? It's so awesome. What happened?"

Tod is much more concerned about my mother's car than he'd probably be about me if I told him what is really going on.

"Nothing, just a part gone wrong," Emma continues. "The computer picked it up and signaled it had to go into the garage right away. It happens sometimes with a new car."

Emma is *so* good at lying — but then, she's had lots of practice with her parents.

As the day drags on I find myself in the oddest mental state. One minute I forget about being sick and everything seems normal. The next minute I remember and everything seems so horrible I want to cry. In fact I do start crying every once in a while and I have to hide from everyone. And then I start to worry about the concert. Maybe it'll be my last chance to dance, and I don't want to blow it.

After school Mother picks me up early so I can eat and get ready for the concert. I go to my room to pack my makeup things up but can't find my mascara. Emma again, probably, I think. Not that she would ever steal. She just uses my stuff and then throws everything in her makeup case without realizing it. I go to Mother's room to borrow her mascara. As I walk down the hallway, I can hear Mother talking to Lorna inside the bedroom.

"What did she say?" It is Mother's voice.

"She was curious, of course. She didn't remember being there."

I stop outside the door.

"I'd been looking through the other albums." Mother again. "I was so upset. I must have had that one in my hand and when I looked through Miranda's albums I left it there."

"You should lock those albums up," Lorna says.

"Oh, surely that's not necessary. Miranda never goes through my things."

"She's going to start to wonder. Don't take any chances. Let me put them in your wardrobe, in the drawer we can lock."

Mother sighs. "All right."

"It'll be easier. They'll be right in your room," Lorna says, "where you can look at them. I'll go get them."

She turns toward the door. I don't know what to do. Obviously I wasn't supposed to hear any of that. Instinctively I take a few steps back. Lorna comes out of the room and I suppose she assumes I've just gotten there. I hurry past her into Mother's room.

"Mother!"

"Yes, dear?"

I want to ask her about what I just heard but somehow I can't.

"I need some mascara."

Mother gets her mascara and gives it to me. "Are you all packed up?"

"No." I pause searching for what to say. "I saw this picture last night in the photo album. Me, in overalls, in front of an old castle. Where was that? I don't remember it at all."

"Oh!" Mother's face turns bright red. What is going on? "That!" She pauses. "That!" she repeats. "Oh, it was so silly," she says in a rush. "Don't you remember? It's not a real castle. It was a picture we had taken of you, by a photographer. The castle is just a backdrop. The overalls were put on for fun, for the picture."

"Really?" I say, trying to think back. "I don't remember it."

"No, well, why should you? You wouldn't forget a real vacation to a real castle, would you? But why should you remember that silly old photo? Now go get ready."

I carry the mascara back to my room and sit down on my bed not knowing what to think. I need Emma. I pick up the phone.

"Emma, want to stay over here tonight after the concert? We can sleep in tomorrow, then go hiking at the canyons. What about it?"

"Yeah, I'd love to. Did you ask your parents?"

"Like they're going to say no. Look, I just overheard the weirdest conversation. I'll tell you when we get back here, okay?"

"Okay. I'll go ask Mom."

Why are there photo albums I can't see? Ever since they found out I was sick Mom and

Dad have been acting stranger and stranger. Especially my mother.

"Miranda! Are you ready? Come and eat." It is Mother calling me.

"Be right there." I finish packing and go to the kitchen. Lorna has made some soup, which is perfect since I can't eat anything heavy. Maybe Emma and I can have pizza after the concert. My stomach is a mass of butterflies. I eat, all the while tempted to confront Mother, but I just don't know what to say. Mother asks Lorna to drive me so she can get dressed and ready.

The dance studio has rented a small theatre at the junior college for the evening. There are no dressing rooms, so when I get there Ms Leanard directs me to the classroom where everyone is changing. We have to use the women's washroom to put on our makeup. Everyone is nervous and excited. I'm terrified. I decide to pretend that nothing has changed. I resolve to concentrate only on my dancing.

Ms Leanard lets each group walk through their number so we can get used to the stage. I go over the steps in my head as I wait in the wings. I can hear the audience laughing and talking on the other side of the closed curtain — I'm so nervous I can barely remember my steps when our turn comes. Then we go back to our classroom and wait as the younger children from the school begin the program. Finally Peter knocks on the door, imitating Ms Leanard's voice as he calls "Places please."

We run up the back stairs to the wings. Ms Leanard nods. The music starts. Rachel makes her entrance. I count. And then I enter. Everything is working perfectly, I can feel it. My body moves in time to the music; I *know* the evil queen's anger. Everyone around me is in sync too — no one trips or loses a beat. There is a hush in the theatre, no one coughing or talking, no babies crying, like time is suspended. I dance, I soar, I fly and then . . . it's over. The applause crashes all around us — I look up from my curtsy to see that the entire crowd is on their feet.

Ms Leanard bustles on to the stage and takes a bow. Then she grabs me and Rachel and Peter and pulls us out for a special bow. I blush, but it feels wonderful. And then I think, if only I could know for sure that one day I'd be able to do this again. Tears spring to my eyes and for the first time since all this happened I feel sorry for myself. Really sorry. But I hate that feeling. "I'll fight it," I vow to myself. "Dr. Mullen says I can get better and so do Mom and Dad. So I *will* get better. I won't give up."

We run offstage, laughing and talking and congratulating each other. We change quickly and hurry to meet our families in the lobby. It is pandemonium. There's a crush of people talking at the top of their lungs. Kids are trying to find their families, babies are crying, girls are shrieking congratulations to their friends. Everyone's parents, and sisters, and brothers, come up to tell me how wonderful I was. I can hardly take it all in. I've danced before at recitals and always had a good response but this is overwhelming.

Dad offers to take the entire group out for pizza and about half of our class, along with their families, agrees. We head over to California Pizza. By the time we get there, two huge tables have been set up for us at the back. We order drinks and tacos and dip while we wait. Emma and her family come along too. Everyone talks and laughs. I feel so happy. Everything *has* to be all right, I tell myself. Everything *will* be all right.

Chapter 6

My parents are so proud of me. But they always are. A little voice inside of me wonders how they would have reacted had I fallen on my face. Well, fortunately I won't have to find out. When we get home I thank Daddy for taking everyone out, then Emma and I go to my room.

Emma isn't jealous of my dancing because she's got her own talent. She has an amazing voice. She's taking lessons now and is considering being an opera star. She's very petite, with short brown hair and big brown eyes — not your typical opera singer. But her voice is *gigantic*.

"You were great," she says as we change into our PJs.

"You really should start to dance, Emma," I reply. She's heard this from me before. "If you could dance, and the way you sing, Broadway would bow down before you."

She grins. "I'll take dance lessons if you take acting. I know you want to!"

"And you know how my parents feel about it. Living in California, *everyone* takes acting. They say all it amounts to is waitress training and they want better for me."

"Do you *always* have to do what they say?"

"How could I even get to acting class," I counter, "if my mom wouldn't drive me?"

"You'd have to walk to the nearest bus," Emma says.

"And how would I afford it?"

"Get a job."

"They'd never let me get a job. 'School *must* come first.' "

"You're hopeless!" Emma exclaims, throwing a pillow at me.

"I know," I sigh, holding the pillow to my chest. "I can't seem to help it." I pause. "But listen, there's something funny going on here." And I tell her about the picture and about the conversation I overheard between Lorna and Mother.

"That is sort of weird," Emma agrees. "Are you tired?"

"Not at all."

"Okay. Let's go and look through your photo

albums. The ones that aren't hidden. Maybe we'll find another picture that isn't supposed to be there. Unless you want to break into your mom's locked drawer."

I grimace. "I don't. But why should I have to? What are they hiding?"

"You know parents," Emma scoffs. "They think the stupidest things are important and they try to 'protect' us. It's probably *nothing*."

"Yeah." I agree, "you're probably right."

"Come on," she says. "I'm wide awake anyway. This'll be fun."

Mom and Dad are sitting in the kitchen talking. Emma and I grab drinks and some popcorn.

"Watching a movie?" Daddy asks.

"Yes," says Emma without a moment's pause. And that sets us both off giggling.

"It's not a movie you shouldn't be watching, is it?" Mother asks, looking at us suspiciously.

"It's a Goofy movie," Emma grins. "We're going to try to decide, once and for all, what Goofy really is."

"Why," says Daddy, "that's easy. He's a dog."

"I don't think so, Mr. Martin," Emma replies shaking her head. "It needs some scientific investigation. There may have been a mixup in the lab when he was made."

Dad smiles but Mother gets up abruptly and hurries out of the room.

"Did I say something?" Emma asks.

"Not at all, no," Daddy reassures her. "Lynda is just easily upset these days."

"Thanks a lot," I say, suddenly upset too. "I'd almost managed to forget this whole thing tonight." I sit down on a chair with a thud, the entire nasty business rushing back to me.

Daddy raises his eyebrows. He's never heard me snap at him like that before. Emma gets her drink and the popcorn. "Come on, Miranda."

I push up and follow her to the family room. We shut the double doors.

"Boy, you're a good liar," I say.

"Practise, practise, practise," she smiles.

I know Emma would never *really* cheat or lie — except to her parents and she feels that's a different case altogether. "And I only do it when they're being stupid," she often assures me. "Like when they ask me what movie we're going to watch. They must think I live on nothing but Disney movies!" But Emma would never cheat on an exam or lie to a friend, for instance. Then I wouldn't be her friend, I couldn't.

I pull out the albums and we start to look through them. There are lots and lots of cute baby pictures, Mother holding me, Daddy lifting me into the air, that sort of thing. And as I get older, the trips, me on horseback, me at my first dance recital. . . .

"Ooh, look at this," Emma exclaims, "our first picture together. It was my birthday party, the year I turned nine. Remember? We had Mr. Cook that year at school and we made friends because he just loved both of us and was always putting us together to do projects?"

"We did that great one on the planets," I say. "Oh. Here it is. Look. My dad took a picture of it."

"I don't see anything odd here," she comments. "No overalls, for instance."

"Do you ever remember me wearing overalls?" I ask.

"You? I don't think so!"

"That's what I mean. But it's not that so much — it's what I overheard. How upset they were. I mean why would they have to hide these other albums? And my mom really looked like she was making up the whole thing about the photographer. I've *never* seen her lie but this sure looked like her first. She was beet red!"

"Why don't we find out?"

"What do you mean?"

"Why don't we look at the other albums?"

"Emma!"

"Well, if they won't tell you — I mean — you *did* ask. You gave her a chance to be honest. And from what you've described, I don't think she was. So, you'll have to find out. After all, it's to do with *you*."

"But Lorna said she was going to lock the photos up," I protest.

"Yes. And where would your mom keep the key?"

"I don't know."

"We'd have to search her room."

"I couldn't. How could I? She'd kill me if she found out. I mean, she's never searched *my* room. It wouldn't be right."

"You've never lied to her," Emma points out. "A fact," she adds, "which your parents don't appreciate enough. A teenager who never lies to her parents. They should give you a medal."

"I've never had to!"

"Until now."

I feel really confused. In a way, she's right — I've tried the honest approach. I've asked Mother what that photo was about. If her answer were true, why would she want to hide the albums from me? But Mother has *never* lied to me, so why start now? None of it makes any sense.

My dad walks into the room. "I thought you two were going to watch a movie," he says.

"We are," I reply, "but we started to look through these albums." Then I have an idea. Maybe Mother hasn't mentioned the picture to Daddy. Maybe if I ask him about it he'll give me a straight answer. Or he might confirm what Mother said about the photographer. Maybe she was turning red like that not because she was lying but for a completely different reason — like maybe she was just hot.

I hate Emma's idea of sneaking around Mother's room.

"Daddy," I begin, "when I was looking at these albums the other night I found a picture of me standing in front of a castle. But I don't remember that trip at all." I don't tell him Mother's version of me in front of a fake photo.

He repeats what I've said. "You, standing in front of a castle. Really? Gee, honey, I'm not sure . . . How old were you in the photo, do you think?"

"I don't know. It looked like I was around ten. And I was wearing overalls. I've never worn overalls in my life. There's not one other picture of me in overalls in all those albums."

"I suppose that's true. Gee," he says again, "I'm not sure. I don't remember exactly. Maybe it was that trip we took to England."

"Daddy, when I was ten we went to Greece."

"Well, it must be that. There are lots of old castles there. You obviously wore overalls and you just don't remember."

My heart sinks — he doesn't say the same thing as Mother. Why?

"Then," I ask, "why did Mother say it was a fake backdrop and she had that picture taken of me right here?"

Daddy pauses and stares at me. "Miranda, if your mother already told you where the photo was from, why ask me?"

I don't answer.

"Miranda!"

"Because I'm not sure she's telling me the truth," I blurt out.

"Miranda! When have we ever lied to you?"

At this point Emma gets up and slips past Dad. "I need something more to drink," she says. Which isn't true but I guess it must be pretty uncomfortable for her to sit and listen to this.

"Well, you never have," I admit. "But now you're all mysterious about everything. Like how you're miraculously going to cure me of an incurable disease, for instance. And I'm worried Mother wasn't telling the truth about the photo because you're right, she never lies, but when she was telling me about it her face went all red, and it looked like she was making it all up. And anyway, why wouldn't I remember it?" I finally stop, almost gasping for breath.

Daddy shakes his head. "We're all under way too much stress, honey," he says. "You're probably reading something into your mother's reaction that isn't even there."

"Then why didn't *you* remember where that picture is from?"

"Miranda. I haven't even seen the picture. It's from years ago. Why *should* I remember? Why should you?" He sits down beside me and takes my hands in his. "I think you're blowing everything way out of proportion. You're really worried about your illness and the operation and instead you're focusing on this silly photo."

Before I can stop myself I say, "If it's so silly why does Lorna want it locked up so I can't see it?"

"What?" Daddy's face goes white and he drops my hands.

"I overheard her talking to Mother," I hurry on, unable to let it drop. "They were so worried about it they were going to lock it and some others up in Mother's room." I realize I'm holding my breath, hoping he has a good answer.

He looks at the floor for a minute. Then he gets up. "I'll get your mother. I don't know what this is all about but I suggest we deal with this together."

"What about Emma?"

"Emma can stay in your room and watch TV there until we've talked. I'm sure she won't mind. I'll go and tell her."

And he walks out of the room, his shoulders drooping, as if he's suddenly very tired.

I know Emma will be mad at me. I think she was actually looking forward to searching Mother's room. But I couldn't. This is better. We'll talk it out. Daddy is right. They've never lied to me. There must be some logical explanation.

Chapter 7

I sit and wait for Mom and Dad to return. How are they going to explain themselves? I flip through the albums. I've been lucky, I think. Really lucky. I've gotten on so well with my parents. I've had all the advantages money can buy — great clothes, trips, lessons. Yeah, I've been pretty lucky, I guess, up until now.

It takes a long time before they both come back to the family room. At least ten or fifteen minutes. I begin to get suspicious again — I have to wonder if they aren't deciding on the same story. Otherwise, why not come directly back?

"Sorry, darling," Mother says, as they come in, "I was in the shower." Her hair is still damp.

You're really paranoid, I say to myself. Stop it. Listen to what they have to say, it's bound to make sense.

"Your father tells me that you've become suspicious," Mother begins without waiting for me to say anything.

"Wouldn't you?" I shot back.

"Yes, yes, I suppose I would," she admits. "But really, Miranda, you mustn't get worked up. It won't help your health."

"Just tell me what's going on, then," I demand, exasperated.

"The conversation you overheard was, well, it was about some . . . silly pictures your father and I took . . . ridiculous ones . . . one day we dressed up in outrageous skimpy costumes and hammed it up . . . it's nothing. Parents don't have to share every silly moment with their children."

I look at her and then at Daddy. They both certainly seem embarrassed enough. And it's true, if they want to act like children I guess they wouldn't appreciate me seeing that. And yet, it still doesn't quite fit with how secretive she and Lorna had sounded. I mean why lock up silly pictures?

"Why lock them up?" I say out loud, watching her closely.

She doesn't turn a funny colour but she does take a deep breath before she answers.

"You know the crazy world we live in. Your

father has a reputation as a serious business-man. What if you found them and thought they were so funny you took some to school and say, Jason took one and showed it to his dad and it ended up all over CNN."

"What's in the pictures?" I ask, still uncon-vinced. "Can I see them?"

"Yes, I've brought a couple to show you." She reaches into her thick white bathrobe and draws out some pictures. Mother is dressed like Cleopatra, Daddy is dressed like Hercu-les.

"These look like Halloween pictures," I say. "I don't get it, what's wrong with this?"

"Nothing," she replies. "But if we're going to be silly we don't need the entire world knowing about it. So you see you jumped to all the wrong conclusions."

"What about me in the overalls?"

"Same thing. You dressed up with us that day, like I told you!"

"But Daddy didn't remember!" I object.

"I forgot, Mimi," he says. "I forgot all about this. We got giddy one weekend and tried on every costume we could from an agency, had them bring them over, took pictures, made up movies, acted out the parts. Do you remember now?"

I try. It sounds like so much fun. How can I have forgotten? Finally I shake my head. "I don't remember."

"You will," Daddy assures me. "The brain's a funny thing, what we can remember and what we can't. It'll probably come back to you. Or maybe it won't. It doesn't matter."

"Can I see the rest of the photos?"

"Some other time," Mother says. "It's late now."

I look at the pictures she's given me. There is actually something a little odd about one but I can't put my finger on what it is. "Can I keep just one?" I ask.

"All right," Mother agrees. "Now why don't you go to your room. It's late. We're tired." She shakes her head. "And stop worrying. It's pointless. There is nothing odd going on." She bends over and gives me a kiss. Daddy does the same.

I take the photo with me and go to my room. Maybe these tumours are affecting me in more ways than I'd like to admit. That thought makes me shudder. What they say is perfectly reasonable. They've never lied to me. I have to stop being so suspicious — and I have to stop Emma from egging me on.

Emma is sitting on my bed when I get there, eyes wide to the point of goggling. She grabs me as I come in and shuts the door.

"I have to tell you . . . " she says, her voice a squeak.

"Emma," I interrupt, before she's finished. "They had a perfectly good explanation. Kind of stupid but it must be true. Why would they make up something like that?"

"What did they tell you?" Emma asks.

I tell her their story then show her the picture. She stares at it. "There's something weird about this picture," she mutters. "Is it your mom's hair?"

I look closely at it. I'd also felt there was something odd — and then it hits me. "Her hair is short. But it's been long ever since I can remember. If you look at all the other photos, since I was a baby, she has long hair in them."

"A wig," Emma suggests.

"Yeah, of course!" I exclaim. "Well, that's an easy one. Although it looks so real."

Emma moves to the bed and pulls a photo out from behind the covers. "This won't be so simple to explain," she says.

"What's that?" I ask.

"You tell me."

I look at it. It is me, a younger me, standing in front of a school. Madison Elementary, it says over the door.

Madison?

"But I went to LaJolla Elementary and then to Juniper Middle," I say. "And now we're at Roosevelt so . . . " Then I stop and stare at Emma. "Where did you get this?"

"I heard your dad come get your mom. They were talking like crazy for ages but I couldn't hear what they said. When they left their room I came out into the corridor too, so I could ask what I should do. Like, were they finished talking to you? Your dad told me to watch some TV.

"They went to talk to you and after a while I got thirsty. I only said I was thirsty before because I wanted to get out of the room while you and your dad talked. So, I passed your parents' room on the way to the kitchen and I saw this album open on the bed."

"You didn't?" I interrupt.

"I couldn't help myself. I had to wonder if it was one of those secret albums Lorna was talking about. And I didn't have to look for the key or anything. So I snuck in and looked through it really fast. There are all these pictures of you but with different friends and it is *not* here because there is snow in some of them."

"Snow?"

"Yeah, snow."

I shake my head and sit down on the bed staring at the picture.

"What does it mean, do you think?" I ask Emma.

"What do *you* think?"

"Well," I say slowly, "maybe this isn't the first time I've been sick. Maybe I've been sick before. Maybe I was so sick I've lost some of my memories. I've heard of that happening. Amnesia. And that would explain my parents lying because you aren't supposed to push an amnesia victim to remember. I saw that on a Sunday night movie once. Or maybe there is a tumour in my brain pressing on something and I'm losing part of my memory and they don't want to tell me and upset me."

"Yeah," Emma says, looking very downcast. "I guess. . . ."

It *is* an awful thought — your brain checking out like that, maybe slowly being destroyed.

I stare at the picture, but it suddenly starts to go out of focus. "Emma!" I cry, grasping her hand. "My eyes. They're going blurry again."

"I'll go get your parents," she says, as she leaps up. She starts out the door then hurries back and puts the picture we've been looking at in my top drawer. "Plenty of time to deal with this later. You have to think about getting better. Don't say anything to your parents now." And she runs out of the room.

Say anything? Why would I? I couldn't care less anymore, I'm too terrified. Blindness — that's what the computer said. Will I be blind before morning comes? And what do any of these details matter anyway? Somehow Mom and Dad have figured out a way to save me. I should be thankful for that and not question what they are doing.

Mother hurries into the room. "Mira," she says, "come on, dear, Dr. Mullen wants to see you right away."

"Now?"

"Now. He's going to admit you to the clinic for two days and you'll have the operation on Monday. Come on, I'll help you get dressed."

"I'm scared," I whisper.

"Don't be, sweetheart. I promised you everything would be fine, didn't I?"

"What about Emma?"

"Daddy will drive her home and he'll meet us at the clinic."

Emma comes in then and hurries into the bathroom to change into her clothes. Mother helps me get dressed.

"Can I come to visit her, Mrs. Martin?" Emma asks as she packs up her bag.

"We'll see, Emma," Mother says. "But she'll have her cell phone and I promise I'll get her to call you first thing tomorrow."

Emma comes over and gives me a big hug. I can tell she doesn't know what to say. I can barely see her.

"Good luck," she says fervently.

"Thanks." I hug her back.

Daddy comes in. He hugs me too. "You'll be fine, Mimi," he says. "I'll see you soon. Dr. Mullen isn't at all worried. He said it was to be expected. Are you ready, Emma?"

"Yes, sir," she says.

"Then let's go."

Mother finishes getting me ready. She asks me what I want in my bag. I say my Discman and my CDs. What good would my books be?

"I'll bring you books on tape," she promises me. "Lots of them. You won't be bored. And soon you'll have your sight back again."

And we leave the house to go to the clinic.

Chapter 8

It's a lonely, spooky drive to the clinic. The streets are dark and mostly empty. Every once in a while other headlights flash past us — to me they look like blurry white orbs suddenly materializing out of the gloom, then disappearing again. And inside those cars are people — probably healthy people, going to a party or returning home from a movie. People who will live their lives out, unlike me. I feel completely isolated from everyone and everything. I start to think about what it might be like to die. Will it hurt? Will it be horribly scary? Is there anything after death or will it just be like being unconscious? I turn on the radio so this unbearable silence is broken. Finally, we pull up at the clinic door.

Ms Yellow Teeth is standing outside waiting for us. She takes my arm and shepherds me down the hall, Mother hanging onto my other arm. Instead of an examining room, I'm led into some kind of bedroom but since my vision is so blurry, I can't see any details. I can make out a bed, and some kind of table by the bed and I see an inner door which probably leads to a bathroom.

"It's lovely," Mother says. "Can you see any of it, Mira?"

"I can see it, but as if there's a fog around everything," I reply.

"Your eyes may improve again," the nurse says, her voice much more pleasant than her looks. "Now let's get you settled. My name is Jean, by the way, in case you've forgotten."

Jean and Mother help me get into my PJs and settle me into the bed. Jean pats the pillows and shows me where the buzzer is, should I need to reach her. "I'm going to give her something so she can sleep," she advises Mother. "She needs her rest."

"Hey!" I say. "I'm right here. You can talk to me."

"Miranda!"

Mother is worried that I'm not being my usual polite self. Doesn't she realize that good manners are not what's important here?

"I'll sit with her until she falls asleep," Mother tells Jean, as the nurse puts a pill in one of my hands and a glass of water in the other. I down the pill without question. I don't want to be sitting up all night thinking of every terrible thing that could happen. I settle back against the pillows and close my eyes. It's easier to have them closed than to try to see through the blur.

"Daddy and I will come back first thing in the morning," Mother says. And that's the last thing I remember.

* * *

When I wake up, everything is quiet. I open my eyes. I can see perfectly again. I must still be dreaming, I think. I push myself up and look around. The room is decorated in deep blue wallpaper interspersed with small yellow flowers. It's very pretty. In one corner are a vanity table and a mirror. Beside it is a closet. The bed is in the centre of the room and I am covered in a deep blue quilt. The pillowcases are bright yellow. The lights are on a low setting. Fresh flowers sit on a table beside my bed, roses, freesias and lilies, sending out a sweet scent. I push the button. I should tell the nurse I can see again.

I lie and wait for her to appear but she doesn't. I push the button again. No one comes. I get out of the bed and put on the slippers that sit neatly on the pale-blue tiled floor. I go to the door, open it, peer down the corridor. No one is there. I decide to try to find someone. I pad silently down the long corridor. I see door after door, all of them closed. I wonder if I'm the only patient here? Didn't Dad say that this was mainly a research clinic? At the end of the corridor the far wall seems to be open a crack, like it's a door not a wall. That's odd, I think, when I hear the sound of crying. I stop dead. It sounds like a young girl or child and he or she is right behind the wall. Where *is* everyone? Why doesn't anyone come and help? Tentatively, I push against the wall, which swings back easily. It opens onto a huge space, all dimly lit but bright enough that I can make out just about everything. At first I'm not sure what I'm looking at, it's all so strange.

The left-hand side of the room looks like a playroom with toys, climbing equipment, exercise machines, big chairs, a bookshelf and a TV. The other side of the room is a small kitchen. In the centre is a kind of bedroom, that is, there's a bed and a night stand but none of it is separated from the rest so the effect is very unusual. Stranger still, there's someone in the bed. The child I heard crying.

I walk softly over and clear my throat.

"Are you all right? I'm trying to find someone here to help but . . ."

The figure in the bed stops crying abruptly at the sound of my voice. A shape rises from the covers, throws them off, and turns toward me. Time seems to stop. I am looking at a girl, perhaps ten years old, with long blonde hair, blue eyes, a high forehead, a little dimple in her chin . . . I am looking at the spitting image of myself when I was ten years old. She stares at me, speechless. Slowly, slowly, now I'm *sure* I'm dreaming, I walk over to her. I reach out and touch her. She jumps back, as if my touch might be electric.

"Who are you?" I ask, somehow finding my voice.

Her eyes are wide as saucers as she stares at me. She gulps for air. Then she grabs my hand and starts to kiss it.

"I will make you better," she says, her eyes fervent. "Thank you. Thank you. Thank you."

"What are you talking about?" I ask. "What?"

"Oh my heavens!" Jean runs up to me through the open door. "How did you get here? Oh, heavens. Come with me, Miranda. Back to bed. Back to bed." She pulls on me and drags me out of the room. I glance back over my shoulder and see the child shaking with emotion.

"Who is that?" I ask. "I want to know! Call my mother."

"I will, Miranda. Don't worry. I'll call her. Let's just get you back in bed."

"I pressed the button for you," I accuse her. "Why didn't you come?"

"I hadn't realized that my beeper battery was low. I didn't hear your page. I'd just gone to check on you and then I saw . . . "

By now we're back in my room. She gets me into bed. "I want to call my mother."

"Of course. You go right ahead. I'll get Dr. Mullen."

My mother's sleepy voice answers the phone. "Yes?"

"Mother! Get over here. There's a girl, she's like another me here. What's going on? Is she my sister? Is she sick too?" And then I have another thought. "Is she the girl in the overalls?"

"Oh dear God," Mother mutters. "Allan, wake up." I can hear her shaking my dad. "Wake up. It's Miranda. She's found number ten."

"What?" I can hear my dad's voice.

Just then Dr. Mullen bustles in.

"Ah, Miranda, aren't dreams funny?" he says. "They seem so real." And he takes a syringe from behind his back and rubs my arm with a little alcohol and sticks me!

"What are you doing?" I exclaim, dropping the phone.

* * *

"Miranda? Miranda?"

I open my eyes. Everything is blurry again but not quite so bad as it was before I went to sleep, the first time. I can see Dr. Mullen pretty clearly. He is smiling at me. Mother's just behind him.

I bolt up in bed.

"Why did you do that to me?" I accuse him.

"Do what, Miranda?" Dr. Mullen asks, looking genuinely puzzled.

"Give me a needle! I want to know what is going on here? Who was that girl?"

"Miranda, this is the first time I've been in to see you," Dr. Mullen assures me.

"You were here last night," I insist. "You stuck me with a needle after I'd seen her — a ten year old version of *myself*." I glare at Mother. "I called you. You know it's true."

"You didn't call me, Mira," she says gently. "It's the medication we gave you before you went to sleep, Miranda," Dr. Mullen says. "You sleep so soundly on it that your dreams are bound to be very lucid. It's normal. What did you dream?"

"It wasn't a dream!" I say. "It wasn't. I saw her! I'll show you her room!" I say.

Mother looks at Dr. Mullen.

"Of course you can verify what you saw," he agrees, nodding at me. "But first let me check you over. Then you and your mother can explore the entire clinic."

He peers into my eyes with his light, takes my blood pressure, holds up three fingers and asks me how many I see, has me follow them with my eyes, and on and on. When he's finished he rubs his hands with pleasure.

"Excellent, excellent," he says. "Miranda, we're going to spend the next two days getting you rested and ready for the operation. We are going to give you a new liver. You're very lucky. We're sure your kidneys, your lungs, and even the tumour in your eyes can be shrunk by our new gene therapy. Maybe the liver could too, but it's beginning to fail and we're not sure the gene therapy will work quickly enough — so it's the organ we're going to transplant. Once you have recovered from that you'll start the gene therapy and I expect you to be back at school, good as new, in no time."

He leaves the room, as cheerful as one of those little 'have a nice day' smiles on those yellow buttons.

"Come on, Mother," I urge her. "You have to see this."

She follows me out of my room. I am in the long corridor but it looks different in the bright light of day. There is no door at the end of the hall, just a wall. I turn back to look at my bedroom. My vision is fuzzy again but I can make out blue wallpaper.

"Are there flowers on the wallpaper in my room?" I ask Mother.

"No, dear," she answers.

"No yellow flowers?"

"No, dear."

I walk across the hall and open the door. It's a small office. I look around bewildered.

"I don't understand," I say in a small voice.

Mother puts her arm around me. "Tell me about your dream," she says. "Was it scary?"

"Yes!" I exclaim.

"You had a nightmare."

Slowly I walk back to my room. "I guess I did," I admit. "But it felt so *real*."

"Those are the scariest kind," Mother says.

"Come on back to bed. You need to eat a good breakfast. While you eat you can tell me the whole thing."

I take one last look around and shake my head. And then I think about the photo, and what Emma and I had been doing. *That* would explain the dream.

"Mother," I ask, "could these tumours be affecting my brain? Is that why I don't remember the overalls or anything?"

Mother looks very sad. "I'm afraid so, dear," she says, "but you mustn't worry. It's temporary. Dr. Mullen assures us there will be no permanent brain damage."

"I wouldn't mind being able to forget that dream," I say to her.

"I know, honey. Come on. Let's get you back to bed."

Chapter 9

I still feel woozy from the pill Jean gave me last night so I'm not very hungry. I drink some orange juice, begin to listen to one of the books on tape, and then doze off again. When I wake up Mother isn't there. Probably went out for one of the zillion coffees she drinks every day. I pick up the phone and call Emma.

"Hi," I say.

"Miranda! Are you okay?"

"Yeah, sort of. My eyes are a little better this morning. But I had *such* a weird dream last night."

I tell Emma everything that happened and how real it felt. When I finish Emma is silent.

"Funny, huh?" I say. "Must be all that stuff you and I were talking about, you know that photo of me in the overalls. Mom thinks maybe this tumour is affecting my memory."

Again silence.

"Emma?"

"Yeah."

"What are you thinking?"

"Maybe I shouldn't say anything. You've got enough to cope with."

"Say."

"I don't know."

"Emma!"

"Okay. Here's the deal. We've been best friends since we were nine, right?"

"Right."

"You've always told me everything, right?"

"Right."

"You never told me about some silly weekend dressing up with your parents. And we used to spend almost every weekend together."

"Well," I answer, "I must have just forgotten to tell you this one thing."

"That's kinda weird, don't you think?"

"What?"

"The one thing you forgot to tell me is the one thing that conveniently explains all those pictures."

Now I'm silent.

"Miranda?"

"Yeah?"

"What are *you* thinking?"

"You're right. It *is* weird."

"And last night," she continues, "what if you *weren't* dreaming. It would explain the photos. Maybe you have a sister or something but she's, I don't know, mentally ill so they have to keep her locked away in the clinic. She sounds pretty unhinged from what you said."

"That would make sense," I muse. "But it wouldn't explain why Mother has different hair in the other picture — unless you're right and it's a wig."

I pause again to think.

"What?" asks Emma.

"Except we look like twins, not sisters. She's *exactly* like me."

"Well, that can happen. Look at the Baldwin brothers or Charlie Sheen and his dad. They really look almost identical."

"True."

"You need to see if you can find her again."

"But I told you, it *must* be a dream, the corridor is different, my room is different . . . oh."

"Oh?"

"What if . . . . no. Emma, we're getting completely stupid here. Maybe Mother is right. The tumour is affecting my brain."

"Just tell me," she urges. "I won't laugh."

"What if they changed my room while I was out. Drugged. The corridor is different because now I'm in a different room."

"Yikes."

"Yeah," I say, "yikes."

"It's possible," she agrees. "There's only one way to find out."

"Don't say it."

"You'll have to explore the clinic."

"But Dr. Mullen said I could. So they couldn't have anything to hide."

"Tonight, when everyone is asleep. Pretend to take your pill. You know, like in the movies, put it under your tongue and swallow. And then go exploring."

"Not alone. I couldn't."

"Invite me."

"How?"

"Tell your mom you want me to stay over there with you tonight. Make a big deal out of it."

"There's no room for you."

"Like they couldn't find a cot or something. Come on. It's a private clinic. Even public hospitals let family members sleep over."

"Family members."

"Well, I'm like your family. At least *try* it.

The worst they can say is no and then you'll have to do it alone."

"Let me see if I can convince my mom."

"Okay. Talk to you later."

"Right. Bye."

"Bye."

I hang up the phone and stare at it. Could Emma be right? Is it possible?

When Mother comes back, sipping her coffee (how did I guess?) I ask her to take me on a tour.

"Sure, honey. How are your eyes?"

"Actually, better." I hadn't noticed, I was so involved with talking to Emma, but they *have* improved. My sight is just a little fuzzy now.

I put on my slippers and robe and she takes me on a tour. The clinic is a large building, made to look like a house outside, but inside everything is shiny and professional. My room is on the main floor along with offices and examining rooms. There are one or two locked doors, probably labs, Mother tells me. The second floor also has a couple of nice bedrooms and a number of labs, again, some of which we can't go into. The third floor is off-limits.

"Why?" I ask Mother.

"That's where they do the experiments and everything."

Maybe that's where I was last night, I think. But no, I'm *sure* I didn't climb any stairs when I first got here. I must have been on the main floor.

"Can Emma come for a visit tonight?" I ask.

"Well . . . I'm not sure."

"Why *not*?" My voice starts to rise.

"I didn't say no," Mother replies, "I was thinking."

"She could even stay over," I suggest. "They could find a cot for her. Remember," I say before Mother can object, "how important your state of mind is when you're sick. In fact, I was just reading about that while I was waiting at the dentist's last month."

Mother puts up her hands. "You're right, Miranda. Company would probably be good for you. But *not* overnight. They'd never permit it."

"But, Mother!"

"No! I'll get Daddy to pick her up after dinner and to drop her off again."

I sigh. I can see that there is no point in arguing. Still, at least having her here will be something to look forward to.

"Can Dad rent us some tapes?"

"Sure. He and Emma can stop on the way here, that way Emma can pick them out."

"Thanks!" As soon as I get back to the room I call Emma with the good news.

The rest of the day I spend in bed listening to a book on tape. It is a really neat story about a girl who suddenly develops psychic powers. Farfetched, I guess, but a lot more fun than all those depressing books about miserable families our librarian keeps foisting on us, swearing they've won every award in the world. I think *we* should get an award for every one we manage to read all the way through.

Dinner is great. Dad brings me my favourite Mexican food from my favourite restaurant. Then he goes to get Emma. He and Mother will go out to eat while Emma and I watch our movie. They arrive with five tapes. We choose *Flubber* and start to watch. My eyes have improved enough during the day that they seem *almost* back to normal. As soon as Mom and Dad leave we turn off the sound.

"So? Can't get them to let me stay overnight?" Emma says, more a statement than a question.

"A definite no," I say. "But you're here now. Come on. Let's wander around. Maybe we can see something."

We go out into the hallway and I show her

all the things Mother had shown me earlier. Jean the nurse is back on duty and she watches us for a while. Finally she goes into my room to change the bedding. Emma and I hurry down to the far end of the corridor.

"This is where it should be," I say.

"But where is the original room you were in?" Emma wonders. "The one with the yellow flowers in the wallpaper?"

"You're right. We should find that first. Let's check all the rooms." We peek our heads into the rooms, one by one. Not all of them, though. One or two are locked.

Outside of that, everything seems to be exactly as it is supposed to be. Discouraged, we wander back to my room.

"Maybe the disease *is* affecting my memory," I sigh. "I mean, you weren't there every weekend, Emma. We don't know for sure it isn't a simple but stupid explanation."

Emma shrugs. "I guess. I'm just so used to being suspicious of everything adults tell me. Mom and Dad always fudge the truth 'for my own good.' Still," she says, "there *are* a couple of locked doors, so we aren't sure the room *doesn't* exist."

We finish watching the movie, then Dad comes back to take Emma home. I'm given my sleeping pills and I drop off hoping I won't have any more nasty dreams. I guess I don't, because the day nurse, Mona, is there when I wake up. My sight is totally clear. She suggests I wash up and says she'll go get my breakfast. I look at my watch. 6:15 A.M.

I have a quick shower but she still isn't back so I peek out into the hallway. All is quiet. A door opens at the end of the hall and Dr. Mullen bustles out. I realize that the room he is leaving is one of the ones that has always been locked before. Maybe, I think, that's where they keep the girl. I take a second look around. Dr. Mullen has gone into a room across the hall and shut the door. I scamper down the hall.

The room Dr. Mullen just left is an office, and it looks like burglars have just finished with it. Papers are strewn everywhere, boxes filled with papers are piled one on top of another, file cabinets bulging with papers are too full to shut. I look nervously at the door across the hall. It's still closed. I sidle into the office and over to his desk. I don't have any idea *why*. I mean he wouldn't have the girl hidden in one of his filing cabinets or anything. I just can't help feeling that everything isn't quite adding up. I glance at the desk. A jumble of papers, logs, and in the middle a large diary open to a series of entries. The date on the open page catches my eyes. November 1, thirteen years ago.

Time of Death: 10:15

I look closer. Lots of incomprehensible medical words. I take a deep breath, check the door, flip the pages. A year later there are more entries, and again, *Time of Death: 1:05.* And a notation. *Subjects may not be able to survive sensory deprivation.*

Who are these 'subjects'? Why are they dying? Are they patients? And what is all this about sensory deprivation? I turn the pages quickly. More and more data. None of it makes sense to me and I'm too nervous to stay in the room any longer. Quickly, heart racing, I try to find the place where the diary had been left open. I can't. I have to get out of the room. How could I ever explain my presence here? Talk about bad manners! I hurry to the door then start walking backwards down the hall.

Dr. Mullen comes out of the other room. I stop. "Oh, hello, Miranda," he says brightly. "What are you up to?"

"Nothing," I say, "I'm just bored."

"Well, dear, you'll soon be out of here." And he hurries back into his office. I turn and run down the hall back to my room. Shortly after, Mona comes in with breakfast. As I dig into my hotcakes I wonder what it is I've just seen. Probably nothing more than a diary of experiments on lab rats. Perhaps I have to accept Mother's explanation — tumours are pressing on my brain, making me imagine, dream, even making me paranoid.

I decide to stop worrying about all this nonsense and to do what the doctor says — just concentrate on getting better.

Another serving of hotcakes would be a step in that direction. I peek out my door to see if Mona is around and I see her stepping into a room a couple of doors down. "Mona," I call, hurrying after her, as I've forgotten my slippers and the floor is cold, "Mona!"

She turns just as I get to the door. Swiftly she moves out of the room and shuts the door behind her, holding onto some clean sheets, but not before I get a clear, if brief, view of blue wallpaper, dotted with yellow flowers. My breath catches in my throat.

"Yes?" she asks.

"I, I, just wanted more hotcakes," I manage to get out.

"Good for you. I'll bring them in a few minutes."

I stand there staring at her.

"Back to bed," she says, "look at you. No slippers."

"Oh, right," I mutter, "bed. Back to bed." And I turn and race back to my room, and to the phone. I have to talk to Emma!

I wake her up, of course, and she is so groggy and I am talking so fast that it takes a few minutes before she can make sense of what I'm saying.

"What are you going to do?" she asks.

"I don't know." I put my slippers on. "I think I'll go on a reconnaissance mission. See what else I can see."

"Take me with you," Emma suggests. "By phone, I mean."

"Good idea," I say, keeping the phone to my ear as I peek out the door. "The coast is clear," I inform her.

"Then go check out that wall again — where you thought the room was. If you were right about one thing maybe you were right about the other."

I hurry down the hallway and look closely at the wall, which I'd thought was a door.

"It's just a wall, Emma," I say.

"Are there any buttons?" Emma asks.

I run my hands up and down the corners

and suddenly I feel something. It's the exact colour of the wall but it's slightly raised and round. I push it. The wall swings open easily.

"Emma," I hiss, "I'm in!"

Chapter 10

Emma answers me. "I can tell you for a fact that you aren't dreaming. Or else I am, too! What's it like?"

"Dim. I can't see much. It was brighter the other night."

"Look for a light switch."

I fumble around until I find the dimmer switch and then I turn it up. Immediately the child sits up in her bed. She stares at me, rubs her eyes, stares again.

"Who *are* you?" I say, walking over to the bed.

"Miranda!" It is Emma. "What's happening?"

"She looks *exactly* like me," I whisper to Emma, "exactly. She's not speaking. Hold on." I come closer. "What's your name?" She just stares at me. "What do people call you?"

"Oh! Ten. I am called Ten. I have been here

ten years. Last year I was called nine."

"Your name is your age? And it changes every year?"

"I am called ten," she repeats. "That will be my last name. I will never be called eleven."

"Why? I don't understand. Who are you? Are you my sister? My name is Miranda Martin. Can you see how much you look like me?"

"I am exactly like you," she says, her voice matter of fact.

"But who are you?"

"I am made for you. My destiny is you. And soon I will fulfil my destiny. Thank you. I have been waiting."

"Can you hear this?" I ask Emma.

"Yeah, but it doesn't make any sense."

"Well," I say, "I'm going to find out what's going on." And I pull the door open wide and yell at the top of my lungs. "Hey! Anybody around?" Then I talk into the phone. "Emma, hang up and call my parents. Tell them where I am. Tell them you won't say anything yet but that they'd better get over here. Tell them they have some explaining to do."

"Okay," she agrees, "I'll do it." And the phone clicks off.

Mona runs into the room. "Oh no! Come on, Miranda, let's get you back to your room."

"So Dr. Mullen can stick me with a needle again and pretend this is all a dream? I don't think so. I know it isn't a dream. I've just been talking on the phone," I hold it up and show it to her, "to my friend Emma. So you see, I'm just going to wait here for Dr. Mullen and for my parents and I'm going to get an explanation."

Mona puts her hand over her mouth and goes running out of the room.

"Hah!" I say to the child. "That showed her."

She looks at me puzzled. "You speak loudly. Why is that?"

"I'm upset!"

"Upset? Upset?" She shakes her head.

"You know, like when you were crying last night. Why were you crying?"

"Oh, I am not worthy. I cannot tell you why I allowed tears."

"Tell me."

"No, then you will not want my gifts. You will think me unworthy."

"I won't. Tell me."

She pauses and looks at me. "I was . . . I cannot explain it . . . apprehensive concerning my non-existence."

"What?" Who taught her to talk, I wonder? She doesn't sound like any ten-year-old I've ever met.

"To not exist," she repeats. "What does it mean? Will it be like sleeping? That's what Lynda says."

I sit on her bed. "Is Lynda your mother?" I ask. "Is Allan your father?"

"I never thought . . . " she muses. "We have never discussed it. They created me. They are my creators. And Dr. Mullen, of course."

"So they *are* your parents," I say. "Look, that means you're my sister! You can tell me what's wrong with you. Are you sick like me? Why are you here? Why have we never met?"

Dr. Mullen runs into the room, panting, trying to catch his breath. "Miranda, please stop talking to her. You'll only upset her."

"And what about me?" I say. "Don't you think *I'm* upset?"

"Of course you are. Please. Be reasonable. Come back to your room. Your mother and father are on their way. They'll explain everything."

"More lies, you mean."

"There's no point in that any more, is there?" he says, pulling me gently away from the child. "Come along."

Reluctantly, I go with him. The girl looks after me with such an odd expression . . . what did she mean by gifts?

I allow Dr. Mullen to lead me back to my room. I go sit on my bed, hugging my knees to my chest. "Are you going to tell me?" I ask.

"Let's wait for your parents."

We wait in silence. I am so confused, so angry, so shocked, I really can't even think straight. It's not long before Mom and Dad hurry in, both of them looking haggard. When they see my expression, which must be pretty dark, they stop dead in front of the bed.

"Well?" I say through gritted teeth. "Will you *finally* tell me the truth?"

Dad sits down on the bed. Mother stands on the other side. Dad tries to take my hand. I pull it away.

"Miranda," he says, "you must try to remain calm. We'll have to talk about this in a reasonable way."

I scramble past him out of the bed. I can't stand to be near to him. "Reasonable? I have a sister and you've never told me?"

"We couldn't."

"Why not? Why is she here? What's going on?"

"She's not well," Dad says. "She's ill. She's mentally ill. So if she said anything to you, anything odd . . . "

"*Everything* she said was weird," I exclaim,

exasperated. "But you don't lock up mentally ill people."

"You do," Dad says, "if they are a danger to themselves and others."

"What do you mean?"

"She, well, she tries to hurt herself. And others."

"She's too little!" I object. "And she was never at home, so how did you find that out?" I pause. "And I *think* I would have remembered Mother being *pregnant*. Or have I just 'forgotten' that too, like I forgot about that picture?" Dad and Mom look at each other, seemingly at a loss for words.

"Miranda, may I speak to your parents privately for a moment?" Dr. Mullen asks.

"Sure." I shrug. "I don't care."

The three of them leave the room. I call Emma on my cell.

"Well?" she says.

"They're still lying," I say, feeling queasy. "They're so bad at it I can see right through them. But *why* are they lying, Emma? I'm really scared. The one thing I thought I could depend on was them and how straight we always were with each other." I pause. "That child is really strange. She said all kinds of things. She calls my parents her creator."

"Creator? Like God?"

"Well, I suppose that's what our parents are. But," I add, remembering, "she included Dr. Mullen too."

"Oh my gosh," Emma exclaims. "What else did she say?"

I'm starting to get a horrible feeling in my stomach. I almost don't want to think about what she said.

"You heard what she said about her destiny. Her destiny was me. I mean, what could that mean?"

The three adults come back into the room. "Is that Emma?" Mother asks, her voice sharp.

"Yes."

"Has she told anyone?"

"Not *yet*."

"Good. Tell her not to. Better yet, let me speak to her." Mother grabs the phone from me. "Emma? Listen to me. If you say *anything* to anyone you will be directly responsible for your friend's death."

"Mother!" I gasp.

"Do you understand me? Good." And she snaps the phone shut.

She starts to talk in a rush, her voice hard, her eyes hard, as if that's the only way she can get the words out. "All right, Miranda, we are going to tell you something now which is bound to upset you. But I think it's better to be upset than to be dead. So, here it is." She takes a short breath. "That girl is an exact duplicate of you. She was created from DNA taken from you at birth. She's your insurance policy. So many children die in car crashes or of some horrible illness, all because they can't get a replacement organ or some bone marrow or something. We, your father and I, were determined that you would not suffer that fate. We were not going to see you die. So we made a duplicate. She was created here, with the sole purpose of donating to you anything you might need."

My knees suddenly feel wobbly and I get so shaky I begin to topple over. Dr. Mullen puts me in a chair.

"Like a liver," I say, my voice barely a whisper.

"Yes," she says, her voice defiant. "Like a liver."

"So you are going to sacrifice her to save me?"

"It must be done. She's not a real person, Miranda. She's a copy. She's been raised in a lab."

"But she talks. She feels. She's afraid!"

"Nonsense. This is the moment she's been waiting for."

I can't speak. I am so shocked, I can't think. A duplicate. A . . . a . . . and then the word comes to me and I say it out loud. "A clone." I start to laugh. "It's a joke, right? It's just a big joke." They look at me in silence. I stop laughing. "You're not my parents," I scream. "You're some horrible monsters. This isn't happening. It's not real! It's all a dream. A dream. I want to wake up. I want to wake up!" I'm laughing and crying and screaming. I think I'm losing my mind.

I turn to Dr. Mullen. "Give me something so I can sleep," I demand. "I just can't stand to be awake any longer."

Dad looks like he is about to cry. Mother just looks mad. I go back to bed and lie down. I want blackness. Oblivion. I can't handle another second awake.

Chapter 11

When I wake up I am groggy but alone. I look at my watch: it's 2:15 in the afternoon. I must have slept all morning. Then I realize that I couldn't have checked my watch unless my eyesight was clear. I lie back on the pillows, exhausted. Everything is wrong. Everything is upside down. Everything I thought was true was a lie. My parents, who I thought were so reasonable, who I never argued with because there was no need, who stressed honesty over all else — they were honest in every little detail and lied about the biggest thing, my life. Suddenly Prospero from *The Tempest* pops into my mind. He used magic to make his daughter happy. It's what Mom and Dad have done. But their magic means someone must be killed. They'll be *murderers!*

That notebook of Dr. Mullen's. Those notations of deaths. Were they rats? Or has he been experimenting on *people?* I slip out of bed and go to the closet. My clothes are hanging neatly on hangers. Quickly I change, pull my hair back with an elastic, splash water on my face in the bathroom to get rid of the remaining drugged feeling from the pills.

I open the door to my room a crack. My parents are standing with Dr. Mullen just outside his office. He is talking fast and leads them into his office. Jean is walking into Ten's room. I may not have another chance. I open the door and run down the hall. I push open the outer door and race down the driveway. I have to find Emma. She'll be just getting out of school. I decide to go to her home.

I realize I have no money, no cell phone, no way to get there. I see a gas station down at the end of the road. I run in and ask the kid to call me a cab. He does, and within minutes it arrives. It takes about twenty minutes to get to Emma's house. I stare out the window, trying not to think. Trying not to panic.

When I get to Emma's house I tell the driver to wait, I'll have to get his money. Just then Emma turns the corner and sees me. She runs over, pays the driver after I explain, and hurries me into the house. Her parents won't be home for hours and her two older brothers are at baseball practice. We have the house to ourselves.

We sit at the kitchen table. Emma gets us each an iced tea. My hands shake as I raise my glass.

I take a deep breath. "You won't believe it."

"I already feel like I'm in some weird Christopher Pike novel," Emma says. "I mean, mad scientists, a spooky hospital, a sister you never knew you had . . . what next?"

"Clones," I say, my voice low, hardly able to utter the word.

"Yeah, right," she repeats. "Clones. That would be the logical next weird thing . . . " She stops and stares at me. "You're kidding, right?"

"I wish I were."

Just like me last night, she is speechless. We sit saying nothing for a long time. "Wow," she says finally.

"Yeah, wow," I echo her, my voice still shaky.

"Gee," she says, eyes wide.

"Gee is right," I say.

She shakes her head and lets out a little giggle. "Gee whiz!" she says. "Gee golly whiz!"

"Golly gosh dear," I giggle back.

Soon we can't stop. We're laughing and giggling and all we can say is stupid words like "oh wow," "oh gosh," "oh boy," "gee willikers," "boy oh boy," "jeepers," "wow," "double wow." We're laughing so hard we both need to stop and drink our tea.

Finally our giggles subside and we are left staring at each other again.

"Wow!" says Emma.

This time I don't laugh. Neither does she. But we can't seem to find the words, either. I mean, it is so out of the realm of reality that we can't take it in. Who could?

"You'd better explain it to me," Emma says finally.

I repeat what Mother told me.

"An insurance policy?" Emma asks. "That's what she said?"

"That girl is just like . . . I don't know . . . spare parts, I guess," I answer.

"To them," Emma comments.

"Right. To them. Not to me. She really *is* my little sister, Emma. In a way. Well, she's really *me,* isn't she?" I stop to think about that. "Does that mean that we'd have the exact same personality too?"

"I don't know," Emma says. "Does it?"

"I don't know either. I mean if we are exactly

the same personality, then, well, wouldn't we be pretty much the same emotionally? I mean I've seen these programs on twins — Mr. London showed us one in biology. Twins separated at birth who are exactly alike — even use the same brand of toothpaste."

"But you make it sound like we're just machines, programmed to react in a certain way," Emma objects. "I mean we're all born a certain way. Does that mean we're going to behave a certain way too? I don't like the sound of that — as if we're just following our programming like a computer."

"What if it is like that?" I ask. "What if, well, what if I could never fight with my parents because I'm just that way? Look at that kid. She'll do anything they tell her. Even die for me."

"Die for you?"

"Yeah, well, you can't live without a liver."

"This isn't good," Emma says, shaking her head.

"I'm not going to let them kill her," I state.

"Then you'll die," Emma protests.

"So I'll die!"

"You don't mean that!"

"What am I supposed to do?"

"You think they'll let you decide? I don't

think so. They're going to go ahead with this."

"No. We have to figure out another way," I say.

"What?"

"I don't know."

Again we sit in silence. What? What can I do? I look up at Emma. "I can run away."

"You can't run away," Emma chides me. "You're too sick. Without treatment you won't make it."

"I'm going to die anyway, Emma," I say. "If I run away they won't kill the child and she'll live, at least."

"Where would you go? You're too sick."

"I don't know!" I declare, frustrated. "But I can't let them do this."

"If she's your clone," says Emma, "won't she get this disease too, in a few years? It's genetic, right?"

"Maybe," I say. "But, they could treat her with this new therapy before she gets really sick like me."

"Maybe I'd better tell my parents," Emma says. "This is too big for me or you to handle alone. We need help."

"I think you're right," I agree. "It would be a relief to tell someone else. And your father's a doctor so he'd know what to do."

"He'd have to report Dr. Mullen," Emma says.

"Good!" I reply.

Emma heads for the phone then stops and looks at me.

"It must be illegal, what they're doing."

"Of course it is!" I answer.

"So they'll *all* be arrested. Your parents too."

"I don't care! They *should* be. I'd rather they were arrested for this than for *murder*."

"But you won't be cured then," Emma says. "You'll die."

"Emma," I say, getting up, "if you won't call your father, I will."

"But that's what your mom meant when she warned me I'd be responsible for your death. If I tell . . . . I can't, Miranda."

"Miranda! Miranda!" It's my dad. The door bursts open and he stands there, face red, sweat pouring off his forehead.

Chapter 12

"Miranda!" My dad explodes. "Are you crazy? You're sick! You have to be back at the clinic." He looks at Emma. "What have you told Emma?"

"Nothing!" I say, before Emma can speak. "I just got here." My first lie. It's easy really. Especially when it's to protect someone you love. Is that why it was so easy for them?

Emma understands me immediately. They're crazy, after all. If they know *she* knows they might . . . what? Murder her too?

"What's going on?" she says, playing stupid.

"Emma, it's a mixup, that's all. I know Miranda told you that she saw her double but, well, she's very sick. Her illness is creating these hallucinogenic experiences which seem *completely* real. I know she thought she was telling you the truth on the phone but she was imagining the whole thing."

Emma nods her head. "I understand," she says softly, appearing to believe him. I realize it's my turn to play the game. I try to look confused. "It's not like that!" I protest. "I'm *sure* it's all real."

"Just come back to the clinic," Dad says. "We'll sort it all out, I promise."

What choice do I have? He leads me out of the house to the car. I see there's a security guard from the clinic with him. They were obviously willing to take me back by force, if necessary.

I look back at Emma as I leave. I don't want to put her in danger. I hope she tells her father. But I have a horrible feeling she won't.

I sit in the back seat of the car refusing to speak to my dad, planning my escape. Next time I won't go to Emma's. I'll go somewhere they can't find me. I won't be responsible for that child's death. When we get back to the clinic Mother is waiting in the front foyer. She puts her hand on my arm. I recoil.

"Don't touch me!" I am so full of anger, no, not anger, *rage*, that I feel like I could kill her and my dad. "So what is this place, really? The clinic where they carry out all the gruesome experiments you fund? What else is here?" Suddenly I remember the third floor. "Yeah,"

I mutter, "what else is here?" I make a dash for the stairs, my parents right behind me. My legs are long, and still strong. They can't catch me. I get up on the third floor well ahead of everyone. I can hear Mother calling, "Stop! Stop! Stop, Miranda, stop."

I fling open the first door I find, surprised it isn't locked. But why lock it? Everyone at the clinic knows what's going on. Everyone but me. And I always do what I'm told. Well, not anymore. A regular office is all I can see. I move to a second door. A lab with a bunch of computers. Then a third room. This one's different. It's full of . . . . I don't know. I walk in slowly. It's full of containers. I move closer. I peer into one of the containers. There is a tiny, tiny fetus. It is labelled, with date and time.

I look around. Of course. Why would Ten, as they call her, be the only one? Maybe she was the only one that worked.

Mom and Dad rush in.

"This place should be burned down. You are evil," I say to them. "Evil."

"We're evil because we want to keep you alive?"

"I don't *want* to be the cause of all this," I scream at them. "It's disgusting. No wonder we never discussed God or religion or anything at our house. You're God, aren't you? Both of you?

"How many more of me are you going to make? Are you going to grow another one after you've killed that child? And then kill her if something else goes wrong with me? It's *murder*," I yell. "*Murder!*"

"She was supposed to be grown just like a vegetable — no brain activity, no brain stimulation — but one after another, they died. Dr. Mullen realized that the human body needs a brain to grow. So he developed a way to exercise her body and her mind and he raised her here. She's never even left this building."

I interrupt. "And you just pretended she didn't exist? That she wasn't *really* your child too?"

"We only thought of her in relation to you — not as a real person."

"No," I accuse, "as body parts."

"Which we never thought we'd really have to use," Dad says. "You should been perfect."

"What do you mean?"

Mother darts a glance at Dad. His colour rises a bit but he goes on, "Just that Dr. Mullen checked your DNA before you were born. And everything seemed fine."

"Checked," I ask, getting suspicious again. "Checked for what?"

"Checked to be sure it was fine," Dad says. "But this clone has to give you her liver. If she doesn't she'll wither away. She's been brought up to believe that is her calling, her reason for living."

I stalk out of the room. "She'll have to find another reason," I call over my shoulder. "Like revenge, maybe."

Dr. Mullen comes puffing down the hallway, obviously having just run up the stairs. "Miranda, Miranda, what are you doing? You should be resting. Oh, this was a bad idea having you here at the clinic. A very bad idea."

"Can we talk?" I ask him. "In *private*." And I glare at Mom and Dad.

"Certainly. Step into my office."

We go into his office, leaving Mom and Dad outside. "They're a little irrational right now," I say.

"Naturally," he smiles, the irony lost on him completely.

"Look, Dr. Mullen," I say, "you need to figure out a way to save me *and* my clone." He starts to protest.

"If you're smart enough to grow a human clone," I say, "you must be smart enough to figure this out." I pause. "I won't have this operation. I'll run away first. Or if you force me to do it you can't force me to live afterwards. I can always kill myself then." He looks shocked. "I mean it. Think of something." I stand up, turn and walk out. I barely glance at my parents as I head for the stairs.

"No more Ms Nice Guy," I say to myself. I hurry away from them. I don't want to look at them. I reach my room and sink down onto my bed. And then, suddenly, I remember the picture. I pick up the phone and call Emma.

"Emma," I say, my voice a croak, "those pictures, those pictures that were me but not me, in the overalls."

"Are you all right?"

"If my mom and dad were lying and we can probably figure they were, then . . . "

"Then," says Emma, "*who* is that in the picture? Ten?"

"It can't be. They've told me Ten has never been out of here."

I'm quiet for a while.

"The photo album," I continue. "I've looked through it a million times. It starts with baby pictures — Mother holding me, right?"

"Right," Emma agrees. She's looked through it many times with me.

"And how does your photo album start?" I ask.

"Well, first there are some really funny looking pictures of Mom when she's pregnant. You know how skinny she is. She looks like a twig that swallowed a moose."

"Yours start with pictures of your mom, pregnant. Mine don't. What does that mean?"

"Nothing?" Emma asks, hopefully.

"It could be nothing," I admit. "But you want to bet if I ask where those photos are they'll make some excuse?"

"I'm coming over there," Emma says.

"It's better if you pretend you don't know anything," I protest.

"They know I was talking to you when you discovered the child," Emma says. "They aren't going to do anything to me. I'll get Mom to drive so she knows where I am. Okay?"

"Okay," I say, relieved. If I ever needed a friend, it's now.

Chapter 13

Mom and Dad come into the room. Before they can say anything I ask them: "Why are there no pictures of Mother when she was pregnant with me?" They don't answer. They just look at each other, alarmed. "Who is the girl in the overalls, *really*?" I continue. "And those so-called Halloween pictures when Mother's hair is short . . . don't you think you'd better tell me everything?"

"I can show you pictures of me pregnant," Mother says. "I'll go home and get them."

"Pregnant with who?" I ask.

"Whom," Mother corrects me automatically. "*Whom*?"

She is silent. I sit down on the bed. It's all starting to make sense. If this can be called making sense. A girl who isn't me but is me. No pictures of Mother pregnant with me. There can only be one logical explanation for that picture. Even though every bit of me wants to stop, now, I can't; I have to keep asking questions, I have to know the whole truth. So I take a deep breath and plunge ahead.

"I have another question," I say. "Why do you both look so young? You look the same age in the pictures of me when I'm ten as you do with your *first child. The one you had before me.*"

Mom and Dad look desperately at each other before looking back at me. Silence stretches out as they seem incapable of replying. I wait. Finally Mother shakes her head and reluctantly tries to answer.

"We've both had some plastic surgery done," Mother says quietly, "so we'd look younger. So no one would question our being too old to have you."

I realize I've been holding my breath. My stomach turns over with Mother's answer, and I feel lightheaded. My conclusion was right. "What happened to that child?" I ask.

"She died," Mother says, her eyes filling with tears. "She died of a brain tumour."

"After she died," Dad says, "Dr. Mullen took her DNA."

"Allan!" Mother exclaims.

"She has to be told the truth," Dad says. "All of it."

"No!"

But Dad ignores her. "Dr. Mullen recreated Jessica, our first child. She's the one in the overalls, standing in front of the castle. He took the DNA and made you, Miranda."

Suddenly I can't seem to quite catch my breath. The room spins around me, I feel I'm falling, falling. I stare at Mother. At Dad.

"I'm not even a real person," I say softly. "I'm just some scientific experiment."

"That's not true!" Dad says. Mother has started to cry. "You're as real as Emma. Just because you were started off differently . . . you're as human as any of us."

"But Dr. Mullen *made* me." I'm trembling — suddenly the image of that little fetus I saw on the third floor fills my head. "I remember when you said he should have known — he must have made sure I couldn't get cancer like she did."

"He did," Dad confesses. "He manipulated your genetic makeup to make you as strong and as healthy as possible."

"So how did I get sick?"

"You think you can control everything," Dad says. "You *want* to — but it seems that your body just spontaneously got sick. Or maybe . . . the genetic code is so complicated . . . some tiny thing went wrong."

"We couldn't face losing another child," Mother wept. "So Dr. Mullen assured us that he'd give us this insurance policy. We thought he meant he'd grow replacement organs. We didn't know at first, he'd been growing other children. And that they'd been dying."

"And when you found out, you didn't stop it, did you? Don't you see how cruel that was? Maybe those infants felt something — loneliness, or fear . . . " I shudder. And then I have another thought. "What else did Dr. Mullen do when he made me? Create someone who is always good? Did he give me my dancing?"

Dad looks so uncomfortable I know I've hit a nerve.

"Well?"

"He may have enhanced your mental and physical abilities," he concedes. Then he gets a wan smile on his face. "After all, if he hadn't made you so smart you'd never have figured all this out."

"You shouldn't have underestimated me, then," I snap.

"No," Dad says, "we shouldn't have."

Mother is still crying. I don't care. I hate

her. I hate him. How could they do this? I'm just a freak. Who am I? *What* am I?

"Could you please leave me alone?" I ask.

Dad takes Mother's arm and propels her out of the room. She's completely out of it, sobbing. "I'm sorry, Miranda," she says as she leaves. "We never wanted you to find out. I'm so sorry. We never wanted you to have any pain. That's why we did all this."

"No," I answer her, "*you* never wanted to have any pain. *That's* why you did it." I run after them and push the door shut. Then I sit on the edge of the bed, staring into space, too stunned to think, until Emma peeks in.

"Hi," she says.

I look at her dully.

"Miranda?" she comes into the room, sits on the bed. "Your parents were *very* upset when I started pounding on the outside door. But when they saw my Mom was with me they had to let me in or it would've seemed suspicious. What's happened? Your mother looked pretty bad."

I'm so miserable I can't speak. I lie down on the bed and curl up in a ball.

Emma doesn't say anything. I'm not sure how much time has gone by when she pats my foot and says, "Miranda, tell me what happened. What did they tell you? Who was that child in the picture?"

I lie on my back and stare at the ceiling.

"Their first child," I say. "Jessica."

"What happened to her?"

"She died. Of a brain tumour."

"That's awfully sad. Why didn't they tell you?"

"Because I'm her. I'm created out of her DNA."

"What?"

"You heard me," I say, sitting up, staring at her. "Mother was never pregnant with me. I wasn't born. I was created. *I'm* a clone."

Emma just stares at me.

"I'm a freak. A monster. A thing. It's why I'm so smart. It's why I'm always analyzing everything. They *made* me smart. They *made* me athletic." I shake my head. "Go home, Emma. Go find a real friend."

"You're still *you*," she says.

"No, I'm not. You should go to the police or something and tell them everything. They can lock us all up."

"No," Emma objects, "I don't want you locked up. I want you better and back at school."

"Emma, I'm *nothing*. Even if by some mir-

122

acle I could get better, I'm just a bunch of DNA programmed to behave in a certain way. What's the point of living?"

"But," Emma protests, "we're all like that. I mean we all get certain traits passed on — physical power, or brains, or something. Like Jimmy, he's a bully, right? And so's his dad. But if Jimmy had grown up *away* from his dad maybe he would have learned how *not* to be a bully. I mean, maybe it's all there, and we're more likely to be one way than another but we can learn to be different. Maybe that's what being human *is*."

I stare at her in admiration. "That's a pretty good speech."

"Well," she admits. "I can't take all the credit. There was this great *Star Trek* on a while ago and it was all about this."

"You and your science fiction," I scoff. I've always thought it was silly. Then I realize what I've said and I burst out laughing. So does Emma.

"Yeah," she agrees, "it's *so* unbelievable, right?"

"Yeah, right," I sigh.

"There's one more thing," she says.

"What?"

"Look, I know you don't believe in any of this

but I do. I think we all have souls. And your soul is your own. It doesn't matter how you were made. You'd still have one."

"Would I?"

"Of course."

"I think my parents should let me die and they can have number ten as my successor. Child number three. Why not? She's exactly like me. They can train her to be another me. They won't even miss me."

"Miranda!"

"It's true. That's what they should do. But before I die I'd like to set fire to this whole place."

"Miranda. Stop being stupid," Emma scolds me. "You aren't going to die. That girl can't replace you. What about me? Who'd be my best friend? What about Susan? She's calling me every hour to see how you are. And you said it yourself; the class couldn't get on without the three of us. They might have to start to work. Come on. We have to find a different way."

Dr. Mullen pushes the door open and hurries in.

"Hello, girls. Well, Miranda, I may have a solution."

"What do you mean?"

"I may be able to save you both."

"How?"

"I could give you *part* of Ten's liver. You each get half. That is, she keeps half, you get half. The liver is an organ that can actually grow. If we give you half a healthy one, a perfect match of course, it should grow to full size. And then I will cure you both with the gene therapy. Well, it *could* work. It's far riskier for you, but it does give Ten a chance."

"We'll do it, then," I say without any hesitation.

"I'll need your parents' permission," he says.

"Tell them that if they don't give it," I warn, "they may have a healthy daughter but not for long. I'll run away, maybe even kill myself. And I'll turn all of you in."

"Interesting," Dr. Mullen says, making a note to himself. "Aggressive. Decisive. Traits I didn't realize you possessed."

"So the lab rat has some surprises for you?" I say sarcastically.

"Yes," he agrees, "yes, you do."

Emma smiles. "See?" she declares. "You are Miranda. That means you get to be just as confused about who you are as the rest of us."

Dr. Mullen nods his head writing as he leaves. "*Very* interesting," he mumbles. "Fascinating."

"*He's* the one who's exactly like the mad scientist in a movie," Emma says. "He's the one behaving according to type."

"Maybe he's a mad scientist clone," I suggest.

"Yeah," she agrees, "maybe he is."

Chapter 14

Emma has gone home, Mom and Dad have gone home, and I lie here in bed, wondering about everything. Tomorrow morning I'll have the operation. I'm not scared anymore. I guess I'm too upset to be scared. I mean, you think you're one thing and then you find out that everything you thought was wrong. I was watching TV earlier and Christopher Reeve was being interviewed. I wondered if that was the way he felt. One minute he was Superman, the next he couldn't even breathe on his own. He must have wondered who he was. But at least he came into this world naturally. He wasn't made, like a computer, put together with a bit of this, a bit of that. It's creepy. Still, I suppose Emma has a point. Once we're alive we're all made up of the DNA we are born with. But how do I know now, when I make a choice, whether it's me or my programming?

Or is there a difference?

The door opens and Jean comes in with my sleeping pill, but she isn't alone. The child Ten is with her.

"Hi!" I say, surprised.

"Hello," the child answers.

"She really wanted to see you before the operation," Jean says. "She's upset. I didn't think you'd mind."

"No, of course not," I say.

Jean puts my pills on the night table. She pulls the big chair up toward the bed for the child, who is dressed in a long white cotton nightgown. The child sinks into it, staring at me the entire time.

"I've just thought of a name for you," I say. "A real name. Ariel."

"What is Ariel?"

"Ariel is a magic fairy. In this play called *The Tempest* he helps save Miranda. It's perfect for you."

"I am female," she points out.

"It doesn't matter. Do you like it?"

"Yes," she nods. "I believe I do." She smiles at me.

"You're very brave to have this operation," I tell her.

"That is the matter I wish to discuss with

you," she says, her face becoming grave and serious.

"Yes?"

"I wish you to take my entire liver. It will be far safer for you."

"But not for you!"

"That is irrelevant. I am unimportant. I live only to serve you. This goes against everything I live for."

I stare at her a moment and then I realize how true Emma's words were earlier. I mean Ariel wasn't *born* believing she needed to sacrifice herself for me. But she was born to be led easily, just like me. Dr. Mullen trained her to believe she exists only to save me. But had she grown up with our parents she would have a totally different view of life. Or if she'd grown up with Emma's family, maybe she'd be more of a rebel because, now that I think of it, Emma's family *loves* her independent spirit, even though it also drives them crazy.

"You are going to have to live for something else now," I say. "I can't accept what you offer, even though it's so generous. You see, you don't know anything else. You can't make a free choice."

"Free choice?" she asks.

"Yes. That's what makes us human beings,"

I answer. "And you can't choose freely because you've been taught to think only one way." And then, I realize how true that is, for everyone. "But that's okay," I say excited, "because we all have, in a way. I mean some kids are brought up to hate black people and some are brought up to hate Jewish people, and some are brought up to hate the government and some are brought up really religious with strict rules." I jump out of bed. "We're *all* programmed in one way or another. We just have to figure out what that is."

She looks at me, puzzled. "It seems to me that would be impossible. If you are programmed you cannot decipher what that programming is. You *are* that programming."

"No!" I exclaim. "You don't have to be."

She looks doubtful.

"We're a big mixup of how we're born and how we're brought up — we have to figure it out, that's all."

"It sounds extremely difficult and complicated," Ariel says. "And I still wish for you to take my liver."

"No." I grin. "I won't. And you'll have to deal with that."

"I feel, I feel . . . very hostile toward you,"

she says in a surprised voice.

"Yeah, well that's because you want to do something and I won't let you," I answer. "Get used to it."

"Why get used to it?"

"You'll be leaving here of course, when this is over."

"I will?"

"Oh, I'll make sure of that. You'll be my new little sister, after all."

"Little sister? You mean a sibling?"

I grin. "Yeah. A sibling."

"This is my home," she says, her eyes full of tears. "I cannot leave it."

"You'll have to," I say. "But you'll like it way better away from here. Have you ever even once been outside?"

"No!"

"It's nothing to be afraid of."

Jean has been standing near the door. She walks up to Ariel and pats her on the shoulder. "Time to go. Tomorrow's your big day . . ."

I take her hand.

"You *are* fulfilling your destiny," I say. "If not for your gift I'd die. Now I have a chance. A good chance."

She still looks doubtful but she nods her head. "I suppose that will have to be sufficient.

At least I do not have to fear non-being at the moment."

"That's right," I agree, "you don't. And maybe I don't either."

"Take your pills, Miranda," Jean says.

She leaves with Ariel and I reach for my pills.

Chapter 15

I've been in hospital for a month. The operation was a success and the gene therapy has worked too. My tumours seem to have disappeared completely. I feel almost normal. Normal enough to be allowed to go home tomorrow. Normal enough to have to decide what to do about my mom and dad and Dr. Mullen.

I'm still not convinced they've told me the complete truth. They lied about everything, didn't they? Until I forced the truth out of them. But I can't monitor what they do here. Not really. And someone has to. Because they were ready to kill Ariel.

So now I have the hardest decision to make of my life. I've been sitting here, going over it all, over and over it, reliving everything they said. And the more I think about it all, the more. . . .

Emma peeks her head in the door. "Hiya!"

"Emma. Don't do that!"

"Don't do what? Boy, you're nervous."

"I . . . I . . . I'm deciding . . . " Should I tell her?

"What?"

"I'm thinking of calling the police."

She sits in the big chair. "What'll you say?"

"I'll tell them what's happened."

"They'll arrest your mother and your father."

"I know."

We are silent for a while.

"Can you *do* that? Can you live with yourself?"

"I don't *know*." I start to cry. "I don't know. But they would've killed Ariel. Emma, what if there are others?"

"Other clones?"

"There could be, couldn't there? We don't know what else they're hiding. We don't know what Dr. Mullen is capable of. Who'll keep them in check? Can I just pretend nothing happened?"

Emma shakes her head. "I guess not."

"But if I turn them in . . . my own parents. They love me. They did all this because they love me." I pause. "I still can hardly look at them or speak to them." I look at Emma. "I *have* to call the police. How could I live with myself if they don't stop?"

And then something else hits me. I stare at Emma. "It'll get out, won't it?"

"You mean, that you're a clone?"

"The *first* clone. The *first* human clone. I'll be . . ."

"You'll be famous."

"Famous, right. I'll have media trailing me everywhere, my picture'll be on the cover of every tabloid."

"You'll never have a minute's peace," Emma says, the reality sinking in.

"Forever. I'll always be the clone. I'll always be a freak." I feel like my brain is spinning and spinning. I don't know *what* to do. Emma sits beside me and puts her arm around my shoulder.

"Fine," she says, her voice determined. "It's time to put all those brains they gave you to work. *Think*. There *must* be another way. If you turn them in you'll hate yourself and you'll be miserable. If you don't turn them in you'll never be able to trust them. There must be a *different* solution."

"You're right. There must be another way." I get up and begin to pace. "They're good parents," I say, "I mean, day to day, at home." I try to think logically. "So the only place they can't be trusted is here, in this clinic. The ordinary clinics are fine, but they can't be in charge of the research clinic," I conclude.

"That makes sense," Emma nods.

"So, I need to get them to agree to turn this clinic over to someone else."

"My dad works in a county hospital," Emma says. "They do research there funded by charitable foundations. Your parents could make this a charitable foundation, and someone else would be in charge then — also in charge of Dr. Mullen."

"And they'd *have* to agree," I say, excited, "or I *would* tell. And they'd realize that then they'd be arrested and my life would be ruined."

"What if they don't agree?" Emma asks.

"They're smart too," I sigh. "They'll *have* to."

* * *

"Miranda. Miranda. It is a new day. Please awaken. It is time for our swim."

I open my eyes.

"Buzz off."

"Buzz off? This sounds like another unpleasant saying."

"Go away! I'm sleeping!"

"But we must do our physical therapy in the pool. Ms Richards will be here momentarily."

I sigh. Having a kid sister isn't everything it's cracked up to be.

"Maybe I'll just skip today," I mutter into the pillow. Emma and I were up last night till 2 A.M. gabbing about Michael Lebowitz's new-found interest in Emma. Michael is extremely cute.

"You must not!" Ariel says. "Only one week more and you may return to school. And I may too. I do *not* want to delay my first day."

And I was worried she'd have trouble adjusting to life outside the clinic. She's thrilled about everything, excited, can't wait . . . I suppose that's genetic too. I have to admit, I've always looked forward to new situations, a new class at school, a trip, whatever. So, we are awfully alike. I try not to think about that too much. About my genetic programming. I'm trying just to enjoy being alive, something only a few months ago I never thought could happen.

I'm still trying to figure out how to forgive my parents. I'm very angry with them. They did it out of love, but that's no excuse, is it? I don't think their reasons excuse what they did. It was wrong. I spend a lot of time over at

137

Emma's now. Her parents seem to know the difference between right and wrong.

Maybe, eventually, we'll get back to some kind of normal here. At least they took Ariel in. And at least they agreed to all my demands. They were very upset with me, to say the least. But they are just going to have to take a chance on life and death. So am I. It was tempting to let them continue, in a way. Then I'd always know I had 'insurance'. But I want to be like everyone else. And I know it's wrong to create people for that reason. Horribly wrong. Dr. Mullen is still doing research on DNA. He has *no* clue he was doing anything wrong. He just does his science and never thinks of where it'll lead. But he's under control now — I hope.

It's a beginning.

"Please awaken!" Ariel says again.

"Wake up," I correct her. "Please wake up."

She throws her arms around me and hugs me. "You are an excellent teacher."

I hug her back.

"And you are an excellent baby sister. I'm awake."

"Good."

"Yeah," I smile. "It is good."

The Author

Carol Matas is the author of many books for children and young adults, including the historical novels *The Garden, After the War, Lisa, Jesper, Sworn Enemies* and *Daniel's Story*. Her contemporary novels include *The Freak* and *Telling*. She is also the co-author, with Perry Nodelman, of the comic adventure fantasies *Of Two Minds* and *More Minds*. Her books have received many honours, including two Governor General's Award nominations, the Silver Birch Award and the Red Maple Award. She lives in Winnipeg, Manitoba.